Up and Up

Up and Up

Erik Sturm

Cataloguing in PID is available from the British Library
ISBN 978-1-9999072-0-4

First published in Great Britain in 2018 by
LIGHTBULB WORKS

To the towns of our childhood. Whether we escaped them or not.

Contents

CONTENTS

Bus Stop Sonnet

November 1996: The Old Mill, Plumstead

"Fuck knows what Rake is up to," said Cezek, knocking back his double vodka and Coke. "The guy's always whinging about something." He only spoke in pronouncements to an imagined audience, only tailoring to the listener if they were alone and he remembered. The rest of the time he would include everyone else in the bar in on the joke with a wink.

"He needs to get a job," said Stacie. She was round and rapidly heading towards obese, but considered herself the adult of the group as she was engaged, yet again, to Gary and she had skipped out on A-levels to work as a floor manager in Topshop.

"I offered to get him work with my brother, but..." Gary shrugged.

"You should all be a bit nicer to him, given what's happened, of course he needs a little time." That was Helene. She was a petite brunette.

"He's known this has been coming all summer," said Gary, shrugging. "He could've done something."

At that point Rake himself wandered in, dressed in

black, with badly-applied eyeliner. He turned his steps towards the table, but paused, and then headed off to the loos.

He was reminded of family parties. People would gather in the front room, talking all nice and polite, then someone would leave to deal with a gripy baby, smoke a fag or take a piss and they would be gossiped about. Not even subtle-like. You learned what everyone really thought in those moments.

And Rake would sit there, cradling his drink, keeping schtum, wondering what the hell the so-called adults thought they were doing. But his mates weren't like that.

Except now he found out that they were. Fakers, just like the rest of them, just like his family. He clenched his fists and then snuck out to the loos. He tried to walk slowly, to imagine himself invisible, as if he were stalking his dinner in Africa. Maybe if he stepped real quiet and kept to the shadows they'd not notice him and he could hear more.

"Rake, what the fuck you doing?" That was Cezek.

"Nothing," Rake muttered. He folded his rangy body into the booth. The patterned seat was torn and the original colour and pattern both unknown and unknowable. The walls were full of sepia photos of toothless miners from before the mine had shut, when the survivors of the war, exhausted by the Blitz, had colonised the area with little box houses. Helene smiled at him. *Faker!* Rake thought.

"You all right?" she asked, reading something in his eyes.

Rake shrugged. "What the fuck I know?"

She frowned. "That doesn't even make sense," she pointed out, validly, he had to admit.

He shrugged and flicked the crisp packet a few times with his finger.

"Another drink?" suggested Gary.

Rake kept quiet for the most the evening, brooding. He stayed there though, until Helene ran off to the loos, her blue eyes reddened by alcohol, unshielded by her glasses, and Cezek joked about spiking her drink. Then Rake snuck out, leaving the rest of the evening to them.

Outside, it was very fucking cold. The wind blew straight across the common and chilled him. It was at the top of the hill and from some directions it looked like the end of the world. The hill fell away behind it and there was just the creepy old mill, the crumbling old school, Plumstead Manor, and the pub. In front of him was the common, but he could see the lights in the distance—the Ship pub, the petrol station, the lone bus stop in the middle of the common where the N53 buses waited before fleeing to London. *What must it be like for the bus drivers sat there at the confluence of two empty and unused roads, nothing but quiet suburbs and the frosty common?*

Rake decided he didn't give a fuck. He strode straight across the grass of the common, cutting diagonally, too cool to use the pavement. He saw a cold bus driver, smoking in the darkness, but he was fifty meters away, it might as well have been ten miles.

He skirted the top of the dip, looking down at the old tin mine. It was strange, this area had been a plane, but some fucker had dug about sixty metres down for profit and that was fine. It was steep-sided and the edges met under the lake at the bottom. There was a fence around it to stop kids getting in, but it hadn't ever stopped him.

But he was damned if he was going to head down there tonight. He broke out onto the main road and decided to follow it rather than head home. He had to think. And, more importantly, he needed to arrive home after the old man was asleep.

He walked and walked. The air was cold enough to mist, the streetlights were ringing with the wind. He felt like an idiot. In his thinking he'd walked a long way. He was in the suburbs of Welling now, and he'd gotten there the long way. He stopped at a bus stop to check the times. He willed a bus to turn up. Now would be good.

"Fun evening, was it?" said a voice. He looked down. A girl—no, a woman—had been sitting under the broken light on the bench. He hadn't noticed her, too intent on the concept of warm buses.

"Not really," he said.

She chuckled. "Ah."

He stared at her.

"You just walking?" she asked.

"I'm fucking freezing."

"You could get a cab home."

"I ain't got no money." He frowned at her. "That's why I'm waiting for the bus."

"I'm not." She seemed not to be looking at him, but to be staring off into the distance somewhere. Then she raised her head. "I'm not waiting for a bus."

He stared at her stupidly, then asked, "But what then?"

"I just needed some air."

"There are nicer places to sit, lady."

"Lise, actually, not 'lady'. How old are you?"

"Twenty-one," he lied, being seventeen.

She snorted. "God, I remember being twenty-one. It's s'posed to be one of the best years of your life, isn't it? It was shit for me, what's it like for you?"

"Shit." He didn't expand on his point, but took a moment to look her over, or, well, eye her up. From what she'd said she was older than him. She didn't look it. She was pretty, with dark hair and dark eyes—they were luminous in the half-light, almost too big for the rest of her features. She was dressed in high-heeled calf-high boots, thick black tights and a short skirt. Her tights weren't laddered and her boots were shiny. Over the top she had on a short, but thick, red woollen coat and a scarf that blocked his view of what she might have on underneath. He allowed himself a moment for the fantasy that it was nothing and then looked away. She was hunched over her handbag, hugging herself, cold even with the coat.

She looked up at him again. "What's your name?"

"Rake."

"That your real name?" He shrugged. She nodded. He sensed that she was waiting for something. "Jane, my name's Jane."

"You just said it was Lise."

"Yeah, you can tell me your real name now."

The bus turned the corner, lit up like a Christmas tree, misted square windows, warmth and safety, a rumble and rush of air. As he watched, it drove up, whooshed as it changed gear for the hill and went past. He looked after it mournfully.

"Seb, me real name's Seb."

She smiled. "Was that your bus?"

"No, mate."

She looked at the sign and grinned. There was only

one bus number on it. "Look... Would you... would you walk me home?"

She didn't look amused as she looked up at him. Instead she looked like Chad had, when he was younger, splashing and kicking vainly, almost drowning cos the stupid fuck couldn't swim. Desperate to reach out to someone, wanting to be rescued. He couldn't understand why a woman at a bus stop would have that expression, but he couldn't watch someone drown again.

"Sure," he said. "I can't leave you here."

She smiled briefly—it didn't reach her eyes—and stood up. "This way."

They walked along dark suburban streets on stained and cracked concrete. Somehow the acidic orange lights only enhanced the darkness. They bled the world of col-our, of life. It started to rain again, a thin mist on the empty trees. When he looked up at street lights, it looked like a horror book cover. They didn't speak. He opened his mouth a few times, but stopped himself, unsure what the hell he would say. He glanced at her a couple of times. She no longer looked like she was drowning, she looked like a normal girl—that is to say, a complete mystery.

They stopped in front of an Indian takeaway. The smell of saucy food drifted out on the cold air. The waiter came and opened the door for them. Jane/Lise shook her head as he recognised her and turned his back—no need to be polite to a non-customer.

"It's here, upstairs," she said.

Rake stepped back. "I'll, er..."

"Come in," she said abruptly.

He nodded. He was so far out of his comfort zone he would agree to anything.

She unlocked the door and he was in a stairway lit by

a single forty-watt bulb. The wallpaper was bubbled from damp and was being shed in large spreads. They shared the narrow stairs with a ladder and piled-up paint pots; he almost tripped over a drill.

"There's a painter-decorator in one of the other flats," she said.

She unlocked a door on the first floor.

"This is me."

"Yeah." Yeah? Could he not think of something better to say?

He walked in. She nodded and shut the door quietly, as if she didn't want to disturb someone. She smiled, now unsure.

"I don't usually do this sort of thing." She wasn't looking him in the eye.

"What sort of thing?"

She stepped in close, reaching up to rest her hands on his shoulder blades.

"What—"

Then she was kissing him, a proper kiss, with tongues, much better than Amy Spencer when he was younger.

She grinned. "You a virgin?"

He shook his head vehemently.

She kissed him again, awakening something within him. Something he knew about, something that no one had ever taken part in before.

She sat on the wide sofa and pulled on his hand. He followed, kissing her. She grabbed his hand and put it on her breast. He pulled back, alarmed, then decided that obviously he couldn't get shouted at when she had initiated. He pulled at her top, giving up and exploring underneath it. She leaned away from him. He was momentarily heartbroken until he realised that she was pulling off her jumper and top. In one fell swoop she was in her bra, her hair hanging free. Rake couldn't believe his luck and decided to ruin it: "But—"

She put her finger on his lips and smiled. "No questions, OK?" Then she put her hands on the hot, throbbing area of his crotch. "You don't need answers."

He said nothing. His entire body was listening to what she was doing. She unbuttoned his trousers and he had no mind, no soul, no body other than this one organ straining under her touch. She pulled down his trousers and massaged his balls and moved her mouth to the tip of his penis. Perhaps he had been waiting his whole life for this. Perhaps his life had been waiting for him. He came, suddenly, violently. Nothing but feeling rushing out of him. When he was back in reality, he realised what he had done. He was mortified, but she was drinking it down, like it was sweet and nice. She grinned at him.

"I'm sorry," he blurted out.

"It's OK." She quirked her mouth up in a grin and he mused about what she'd done. "I hope there's plenty more where that came from."

Rake wasn't so sure, but as she wiggled out of her clothes he felt the stirrings again. She grabbed his hand and put it where he had never put his hand before, where his younger self had dreamt about putting it.

"Try touching me there..."

"Like this?"

"Like this, like that, like that, oh, like that..."

Her hips bucked and she rolled her head back. He wondered if she was faking it. He had read magazines about this, how to tell if women were faking. It was something to do with wetness... He couldn't remember anything else, but there had been something about using your tongue, only real men could handle that.

He bent forward and explored with his tongue. Jane was gasping now. He was writing the alphabet with his tongue, and after that, he tried spelling the stupid phrases from Shakespeare he'd had to learn. He hadn't given a fuck about it at school and here he was, spelling out Hamlet's bloody speech. She squirmed and bucked, finally pounding her pelvic bone into his teeth. That fucking hurt.

He pulled away. She was giving him a watery-eyed stare.

"Fuck, that was good. I thought you were a virgin."

"Shakespeare's good for something."

"What?"

"Shakespeare. I was spelling it out on your..." He couldn't bring himself to say 'clitoris' and blushed instead.

"What from Shakespeare? *Romeo and Juliet*?"

"Yeah," he lied.

"You studying English?"

"Summink like that."

She sighed back, leaning against him, her arms around him, but he wasn't in the mood to talk, he was in the mood to go all the way. He rocked against her. She wiggled herself against him, driving him to the very edge.

"You want me?" she whispered huskily.

His mouth was dry. What could he say? He nodded, unable to think.

She grinned and pushed him onto his back and climbed on top, driving herself down onto him. He almost shouted but didn't. She rode him again and again, every thrust feeling like the end of the world, pushing him to the limit of sanity and back. She squeezed, she pulsed, she held him on the very tip, slowing just as he was about to... then speeding up again when he was back from the brink, driving him back and forwards, coming herself, he felt it flood out of her, over him until eventually, with a cry, she arched her back and squeezed with something deep inside of her and he felt himself answering, then everything, all life, all light, all reality flooded out of him into her.

Then they were breathing, just breathing, fast, but slowing. She slumped against him, sticky with sweat. Their ribcages bashed with every breath.

She curled up against him, her head nestled on his shoulder. He felt her shudder and cry. Not sure what the hell to do, he found himself putting his arms around her, wondering if this was normal or if he was so awful in bed.

Finally, she lifted her head and smiled. Her eyeliner had painted black rivulets and tributaries. "Sorry, it's just, y'know, the release, the tensions, sometimes... y'know, I cry."

"Right." *Women are fucking weird.*

She stood and smiled at him. "Er... tea?"

He nodded and tried not to feel uncomfortable about the fact that he was completely naked and on a stranger's sofa.

She put the kettle on and padded off to a bedroom and returned in a dressing gown. He sighed and slumped back. The sofa was orange, one of the strange, huge ones that go round a corner. He hadn't cared to notice before, but the room wasn't great. There was a yellow streetlight shining in the window and a pulsing red light from the adverts on the corner shop next door. Together with the Christmas tree lights, it was colourful at least. The walls were peeling magnolia, the carpet so old that it might as well have been paint, but the place was tidy and laid out with girly things like pot plants, wine bottles with candles in the top and cutesy ceramic ornaments.

As he squashed himself into the corner bit of the sofa, he put his hand in an ashtray full to overloading with the remainders of roll-up cigarettes. Swearing, he put that on the low, white vinyl coffee table.

Jane had her back to him, in the kitchen part of the main room. He heard the kettle switch off, then her pouring water into cups. He wiped his hand on the white throw, then folded it over to hide the ash stain and covered himself with the rest of it. She walked back in and put the tea down in front of him.

He stared at it, wondering what the hell he was supposed to say.

"Would you..." She had the drowning look again. "Would you stay here tonight?"

———————————

That morning, Rake prepared lots of excuses for his parents for why he hadn't come home, and was mildly annoyed that they hadn't noticed. He spent the day doing nothing much except musing on the fact he had had sex and wondering when he would see Jane again. The concept that he might not hadn't occurred to him.

One evening later, he was chilling in his room, listening to Guns'n'Roses, when his sister yelled up the stairs, "Bruv! There's a girl here to see you!" He half fell, half flew down the stairs and came face to face with Helene. She had her face screwed up in that funny way she did when she was concerned. His sister giggled from behind him.

"That's not a girl, that's just Helene!" he shouted at her as she pounded up the stairs.

Helene looked kinda awkward. Then she recovered by pretending to be concerned about him. "Are you OK? You were well quiet yesterday," she whispered, but Helene wasn't all that good at being subtle. "Did your parents bawl you out about—"

"Mum! I'm going out!" he hollered. "Let's go," he said, opening the door.

"Where we going?"

"For a walk."

"It's dark."

Rake growled. "Just move it, would you?"

He practically marched her down the drive, ignoring his mother's shouting about dinner or some such thing. She made her final point and slammed the front door as an exclamation mark.

"Are you in trouble?" asked Helene, her eyes wide.

"Fuck's sake, I nearly was. You can't just come round my fucking house and tell them everything."

"What, you mean they don't know?"

"Of course they don't fucking know, my dad would kill me!"

"If they find out, you can always come stay at mine. Me mum likes you, she'd let you stay, maybe even rent free, I mean if you was going to get murdered..."

"Well, he won't really murder me." Rake was pretty sure. "I s'pose me mum might..."

"Oh."

Rake grinned, suddenly remembering the night spent holding Jane in his arms. He wasn't a scared child no more, he was a man. "It don't matter."

"You'll have to tell them, you know."

He shrugged. "Fuck 'em."

They arrived on the common. They walked past the running machine, a metal cylinder with a bar above to hold on to as you ran on the cylinder. They stopped on the step 'machine', six wooden benches arranged so you could run up and over them repeatedly. There was a half-a-foot step up from bench one to two to three, then you ran down the other side. Next to it, planted like a care sign for plants, was a cartoon instruction showing how to run up and down. It was put in place for unemployed people to use to work out. Perhaps it was cheaper for the local council to build this shit rather than offer gym sub-sidies. Rake mused that perhaps he should use the assault course—after all, he was now actually unemployed...

Rake and Helene sat on the top of the steps. In front of them in a patchwork of darkness and orange spread south-east London, arcing down towards the river, all twinkling yellow lights like stars taken out of a movie and brought to earth. In the distance, the factories of Essex; to the left, the rest of Greenwich and the skyscrapers of the Dock-lands spearing the clouds beyond that.

"You were in a right mood at the pub last night, what 'appened?"

Rake grinned at her. "I got laid."

Her eyes boggled. He grinned widely.

"Oh!"

"Yeah."

"Really? You're not shitting me?"

"Yeah."

"So you're not a virgin no more?"

He grinned and nodded. "Nope!"

"Oh. Who was she? Or was it a he?"

He glared at her. "I ain't fucking gay! And she is called

Ja—Lise."

"Jay-Liseh?"

"No, just Lise." For some reason he didn't want Helene to know Jane's real name.

"Where'd you meet?"

"At a bus stop. On the way home."

"I never meet interesting people at bus stops, just creepy old guys."

Rake shrugged. What the fuck did he care about Helene's love life?

"So then what?"

"I went back to hers and... y'know."

"Oh."

"You do know, don't you? You're not a virgin?"

Helene raised an eyebrow in an 'as if' expression and then blushed.

Rake chuckled.

"Just don't ask me about my first time."

"Why?"

She shrugged like a fir tree losing melting snow. "It doesn't matter, all right?"

"But was it good?" He grinned. "Was there any Shakespeare?"

"Shakespeare? What the fuck are you on about?"

"Y'know, *Hamlet*."

"*Romeo and Juliet*'s more romantic."

"That's stupid. They just fuck everything up and commit suicide together in such a dumb way. That's not romantic, that's two people on a downward spiral with personality issues."

"You know so much about it, anyone would think you'd passed English."

"Oh, shut up."

They sat and stared at the lights. Helene shivered and pulled a packet of cigarettes out—Marlboro Lights, the shit that girls smoked. She even went so far as to smoke menthols. He'd been told that real smokers didn't smoke menthols.

She offered one to him out of some sort of faked-up Christian charity. So he took one. She frowned.

"You owe me. Those are pricey, you know."

"Your mum know her little choirgirl smokes?"

She shrugged and pulled out her lighter, cupping her hands around it as if it were warm rather than just a bright flame. It took her three attempts to light it. Helene always used lighters until they were nothing but gas vapours. Then she would buy a new one and fuck with the mechanism, moving the adjuster up and down and up and down until she broke it enough that the flame was six inches high. That was why the girl went through lights and six for a pound wasn't really a saving for her. She'd done it once with Cezek's lighter at the bowling alley. After a few Southern Comforts and Cokes she'd thought it was funny. He'd burnt his eyebrows, the hairs black and curly from where he'd leant in over a cigarette. Then he'd punched her in the boob while she laughed. Then she wasn't laughing and Rake was left wondering if it was the same as punching a guy in the balls. It was how those two flirted. They'd probably kill each other if they tried to mate. He thought that might be for the best.

Helene was staring at the distant streetlights, her cigarette hanging louchely off her right hand, her forearm balanced on her knee. Or maybe she was watching the smoke rise in the cold air and purposefully posing like some actress in those stupid French films she watched, and he swore she only watched them because her parents had decided to call her Helene rather than something sensible. She was no more French than Cezek's mother was sure her son was Polish.

"It wasn't really my first time, I guess, just my first kiss, I s'pose..."

He watched, wondering if she was going to draw on the cigarette that was so expensive.

"Then there was the first time I was touched... well, y'know, then Italy..."

Rake shrugged. The first time he reached third base and the first time he was fucked were one and the same, so how could he understand?

"Then Chad."

"I thought he was your first."

"Yeah..."

The cigarette was just burning, the cherry fighting the cold wind, uncaring that Helene didn't seem bothered by its struggle.

"He was the first guy I slept with..."

The cherry was close to her fingers now. He wondered whether she felt it.

"Who was the second?"

She stared at him.

"There was no second." She lifted the ciggie and seemed confused that it was almost at the filter. Taking a drag of burning cotton wool, she sighed, blowing the smoke out her nostrils in a way that only real smokers could do. Then she flicked it away, the cherry describing an arc in the cold night.

Brass and Gilt

2008: A Bar in Soho

It was the sort of place Rake detested. He didn't understand why the other guys from the bank went so mad for it. He was up for a good time, like anyone, and he did a little coke, like anyone, and he was more than happy to admire the female form, but not like this. The club had a bad rep, it was seedy, but on the up, and weren't they all on the up and up?

The prozzies/dancers were poor Eastern European types. *Had they come here expecting this sort of life? Had they left young farmers, or whatever they had back home in Romania, to try to bag a rich English husband, and ended up here?*

Rake didn't want to know. He could tell more than enough of the truth from their eyes.

He knocked back another forty-quid champagne cocktail. *Why the fuck did they have to come here? What was wrong with Spearmint Rhino?* The girls were there through choice—sure, they were all after turning a quick fuck into an all-expenses-paid WAG lifestyle, but at least they weren't damaged goods like these girls.

Rake had had enough of damaged goods.

Tony leaned forward and snorted a line of coke off the table through a fifty-quid note. Then he leaned back and made various disgusting snorting noises like this was going to be the time he lost his septum and grinned.

"Not as good as snorting it off a beautiful girl's belly, but here at least I can look at one!"

And that was why, Rake guessed: the seedy club run by fucking Russian gangsters allowed them to do their coke on the tables rather than in the loos. No matter how gold-plated the urinals, they were still the bogs.

It was the sort of place where you didn't need to go to the bar, but as Tony called over a girl who couldn't have been more than sixteen and got her to do a lap dance for him, Rake got up. Somehow Tony only saw her jiggling butt and missed the desperation. Rake leaned on a brass bar—he guessed that the owners thought people might mistake it for gold in the dark. He was watching the bartender shaking his next drink, or rather he was watching her boobs shaking as she did so, when he heard a familiar laugh.

Almost like horror he turned his head, hoping against hope that it wasn't him. Too late. His old... mate... Cezek was striding towards him. Rake stared unmoving, hands fisted, fully expecting to be hit or stabbed, cursing his luck that he'd gone to such a divey place that he'd bumped into the fucker.

"Rake, me old china, what the fuck you doing here?" And with that Cezek was thumping him on the back companionably. Rake was too slow to hit him back and by the time it occurred to him, he'd realised that Cezek wasn't being sarcastic.

"Fuck," said Rake.

"Fuck? I ain't seen you for ten years an' the first thing you say is fuck?"

"How are you, Cezek?" sighed Rake.

"How am I? I'm fucking rolling in it! I am a bona fide million-fucking-aire! How's that for a bootheel from the arse of the world?"

"Arses don't wear boots."

"What about you? What the fuck you doing in such a high-class establishment?" Cezek wasn't joking.

The bartender stopped shaking the drink now she realised that no one was looking, gave Rake a 'I'd fuck you for a grand' grin and poured out the whitish-fizzy drink ever so slowly, leaning forward so he got a good view of her rack. She spilled some on her cleavage, and she looked at him as she wiped it off with her finger and licked it.

"Hey, you're paying for that," remarked Cezek to him.

Rake shrugged and handed the bartender a hundred-quid note. "Get one for yourself, love."

"Thank you, sir," she bubbled, and Rake frowned when he clocked her accent. He had thought that she was a local, not a sex slave, as mixing drinks was definitely a skilled occupation.

"I'll have the same, his tab," said Cezek.

Rake glared at him. "I thought you were rolling in it."

Cezek shrugged. "You not gonna buy me a drink? You don't think you owe me, for old times' fucking sake?"

Rake sighed and handed the bartender another fifty. "Don't bother with the dance for this guy, he's gay."

Cezek scowled. "Hey." He turned to the bartender. "I'm not gay. That's what we said about him at school. Hey!" added Cezek over his shoulder as Rake walked off. He turned back to the bartender. "Fucking hurry up, and add the wiggle."

"But the Rake, he say—"

"I don't give a fuck what Rake says, he your fucking boyfriend? No? So do what I say."

Rake squeezed past Tony and the girl he was licking and sat down. It was four-fucking-am and he was due at work at five-thirty.

Red Bull just wouldn't cut it.

So Rake did himself a line, the coke ringing through his system and waking him up into some higher state of wakefulness, like he was a superman or something and could see everything and know everything.

Cezek would follow him over, it was inevitable. Rake gulped the champagne margarita. It was acidic, rough, limey and bubbly—it went perfectly with coke.

And then Cezek was there. "Rake, so what the fuck do you do?"

His mates stared at Cezek. "You're s'posed to pull girls here, Rake, not fucking plebs."

"I ain't fucking gay!" said Cezek, his hands fisted and ready to throw a punch. "I know this fucker from school, all right?"

The Tank, as he was known, nodded. "Well, a fucking school reunion, is it? Rake, you know any hot chicks from school? Any supermodels?"

"As if," said Rake.

"I know you," said John. "You're Cezek Hitch, aren't you?"

Cezek grinned. "Yeah, I fucking am!"

John looked at Rake, who was floating in his own world where all his senses were singing. "Can you set me up a meeting?"

"What for?" asked Cezek.

John grinned. "I got some deals that might interest you, Mr. Hitch. Who currently manages your investments?"

"I manage my investments." Cezek stared at Rake. "You're a fucking banker?" Rake didn't respond. "A banker! Ha! I always said you were a banker at school, or was it wanker? Hah hah hah!"

"Just fuck off, would you, Cezek?"

"Fuck off? Hah! That's no way to speak to your old mate."

Rake glared at him. "What the fuck you want? Hmmm? A fucking parade?"

The other bankers stared at Rake.

"A hah hah hah hah," laughed Cezek, after a semibreve during which he'd decided that Rake was being funny. "A parade. Fuck, yeah. Why the hell not." He grinned at them all. "Which bank is it?"

John was quick and got his card out of his pocket. But Cezek noticed Tony's on the table from where he'd used it to lay out the lines. It was a favourite trick of Tony's. He liked to pass it on to his most innocent of clients.

"Lehman Brothers," read Cezek. "Not even fucking heard of it."

"Go to Barclays," said Rake, then he licked his tingling teeth.

Cezek grinned and waved the card at him. "I reckon I could do with playing the markets a bit, y'know, what would people think if I just kept all my money in bricks and mortar? S'posed to be as safe as houses! Hah! I've seen some houses that are only standing through luck and sellotape." He looked over at Tony. "Fucking bankers," he said, jerking a thumb at him and laughing. "I'll drop by and see you," he said to Rake. "We got old business."

"Cezek, it's nice we met in a dive club and all, but that was just chance, so why don't you fuck off back to your slums and screw a few more losers out of another couple of pence? You don't need investments, you need a fucking therapist."

"Y'know, Rake, you're a right fucking arse when you're on coke." Cezek laughed. "A right fucking arse."

He downed his drink, got up, sniffed along the edge of the business card and then saluted them with it. As he walked off they could hear him repeating, 'Rake, a fucking banker!'

"You know Cezek Hitch?" asked John.

Rake sighed. "He's an arsehole."

John laughed. "All our clients are arseholes."

Radio Song

1996: Rake's house, Plumstead Common

The radio started. Music, REM, *Night Swimming*. Not the best track to wake up to. It didn't really fit with the morning ambience. As the last of the hypnotic piano undercurrent died away, the DJ came in, all abrasive personality and in-your face 'character'.

'Now it's time for our live prank call five minutes! This is for Steve of Coltenshire, we got this a few months ago from his mate Dave Bradford. It says in your letter, Dave, that Steve has been boring you rigid with his plans to take his kids on a trip of a lifetime to Disneyland over Christmas...'

Rake lifted his hands above his head, blocking out the light from the attic window. It needed a blackout blind. He had been promised a blackout blind when he'd agreed to take the attic. It didn't have one. In the summer he was accustomed to sleeping with his head under the cover to try and block out the four am sunrise. That and the wasps from the wasps' nest in the awning. But this was eight am.

'Let's put the call through now.' Ringing tone.

'Huh... hello?'

'Steve! It's Bob Delany from Brompton Holidays. I'm just calling you up to let you know that, due to an unforeseen error, your holiday this Christmas has had to be cancelled. We've not had the take-up and...'

Rake sat up, looked around the room, taking in the uncovered fibreglass ceiling and the mess he'd overlaid the room with. As was his habit, he glanced over at the wasps' nest in the corner, but they were only active in the summer and mean in autumn. He slumped back down again and pulled the cover over his head anyway.

'Holiday? You're from the holiday company?'

'Yes, Steve, and we're sorry that your holiday's been cancelled, we've got one space left for a family of four, that same week, but that package is two thousand pounds more—'

'Who is this? Do you think this is funny?'

'Hah! You're too smart for us, this is Dr. Feelgood of Morningside Radio, ha ha ha—'

'Why the bleep are you doing this? Who the bleep would...'

'Please, you're live on Morningside Radio! We're having to bleep you out.'

There was a silence.

'My wife and children were killed in a fire a month ago and... you...'

'Uh...'

There was a silence, a ringing, buzzing silence. Rake had never known the radio to be so silent before. Then, suddenly the jarring tones of Take That and Lulu burst out.

"Fuuuuuuck!" whispered Rake. He visualised the panic of the radio people, slamming on the next track. He thought about the radio DJ's worry, well aware that he couldn't ever understand how Steve was feeling.

"Rake! Get up! You'll be late for school!" hollered his mother.

He waited for Lulu to give up on resuscitating her pop career, to see if the DJ would offer any words of comfort or apology. Meatloaf: 'I would do anything for love...' His mum yelled. Adverts, the news...

'Good morning to everyone just joining us, it's now eight o'clock..." The DJ didn't sound troubled, he sounded like he was grinning, perhaps a rictus grin. Rake hoped so. The DJ prattled. More shit music. Rake pulled on his trousers and headed downstairs.

"You'll be late!" said his mum. She was a whirlwind of activity. He swore that as she moved in the mornings she was orbited by her Filofax, her Nutrigrain bar, her cheap coffee, her lipstick, her purse, but maybe it was just an illusion. He was pretty sure that his mother didn't have telekinetic powers.

"Double free, first period," he muttered as an explanation as he poured some sort of cardboard flakes from a cardboard box. He doused the foodstuff that purported to be fortified with vitamins and iron in semi-skimmed milk and watched the flakes drown.

"You should still be at the school, they mark your attendance. You'll never get a job with a bad attendance record." Whilst berating him she had lined her eyes in kohl, applied brown eyeshadow with a dab of blue in the centre, to make her eyes look blue apparently, and gulped half a cup of cold coffee. Rake felt almost dizzy at her speed.

"OK, the rest of you, in the car now!" She shuffled his brother and sister out. His father had already moved himself into the vehicle and was patiently waiting whilst smoking a roll-up. The door slammed and Rake chewed his first mouthful of cereal as his mother left.

Rake bathed, dressed and settled down to TV watching. The clock blinked ten-thirty. He cursed his mother for the fact that he had to get up so early just to keep up the pretence for her. *Friends* wasn't working out for him. He'd seen the episode about a hundred times and now used it as some sort of psychic medicine, but he couldn't laugh as his mind kept returning to the morning's radio program.

He went for a walk. He had meant to go to the woods. He'd always felt happy there—he remembered the sun shining through the leaves, warm orange sunlight of summer, leaves like shards of glass. But it was nearly December, the air was cold and he wasn't really dressed for it. Too stubborn to turn around, he just walked and smoked. He wanted proper cigarettes but made do with tobacco and papers he'd stolen from his old man. He flicked the butt towards a bin, missed, but left it in the curve of the curb so the street cleaners would have something to do for their money, and rang on Jane's doorbell.

It was, it seemed to him, a complete accident that he had turned up there. He didn't bother to recall that he had walked directly to hers.

"Huh... hello?" she asked.

He stared at the intercom, wondering why he found her greeting disturbing. "It's Rake, I mean Seb."

There was a silence whilst he studied the intercom. It was rusted around the edges.

"What do you want?"

Rake frowned. "To see you, of course, isn't it obvious?"

There was a sigh, or maybe it was the intercom. "Tea,

yeah? I'm not promising nothing but tea."

Rake grinned. "Tea would be grand."

"Give me a minute to put me face on."

Rake nodded enthusiastically and then realised that she couldn't see it. "Sure."

She took ten. Rake wondered how any woman could take ten minutes to put make-up on. He smoked another rollie.

"You still there, Seb?" went the intercom.

"Yeah. And cold."

The door buzzed. She didn't come down to let him in. He had to find his way up to her flat by himself.

He paused on the threshold. Green glass shards surfed the carpet. There were purple stains on the wall where the wine bottle had been thrown and the videos were no longer on the MFI shelving unit, but scattered on the floor.

"What the fuck happened?"

Jane slunk out of the bedroom. She had a black eye, but she'd covered it with that funny stuff that women like to paste on their faces. The orange gloop couldn't stop the puffiness from showing. She'd reparted her hair to hang down more on that side and she fiddled nervously with the fringe. It didn't cover the bruising.

"What happened?" asked Rake. Her expression plainly said that what Jane wanted was for someone to take her in their arms and say everything was all right, but Rake was too shocked to even think of that. "You have a fight?"

"Something like that." Her voice was brittle and bright. She walked past him into the kitchen area. "Tea?"

"Tea? Your flat's been trashed and you're hurt." She

stiffened. "Why the fuck do you want tea? We should call the filth."

She rushed around the counter, her arms thrust out as if she were falling. "No. No police."

Rake eyed her and nodded. "Sure, OK, no filth. Bastards probably won't catch the fuckers anyway. Were you robbed? Was anything taken?"

Her hands worried up near her throat like starlings on a telephone wire. "I wasn't robbed."

"So what happened?"

"It was..." She gripped the Formica counter-top. He could only see her eyes through heavy lashes. "It was my boyfriend," she said in a small voice.

Rake gibbered—it was a full-body gibber. He shook and took a few steps back. "Your boyfriend? You have a boyfriend?"

She looked up then. "Yes. Sorry."

"Sorry? What the fuck?"

"It's OK, he doesn't know about you, it wasn't your fault."

"What? Who cares what he knows about? Why didn't you tell me you had a boyfriend?"

She put her hand up to cup her swollen eye. "You didn't ask."

"Didn't ask? Are you supposed to ask? Am I s'posed to ask every girl if she's got a boyfriend before—"

"C'mon, like you've never cheated on anyone."

He stared at her.

"Oh." She looked down again, tugging the fringe down. "I'm sorry." She shook her head. "I'm so sorry, I'm a terrible person." And with that she put her head in her hands and started weeping, even though it must have hurt her eye. Rake crossed the apartment in two bounding strides and hugged her.

"Hey, hey, it's OK. I don't mind, it's OK."

She shuddered and just cried on him for a long while. Had she looked up she would have seen that Rake was far out of his depth and treading water badly. He stared at the wine bottles and wondered what you were supposed to do when you fancied someone else's girlfriend and that person plainly didn't deserve her.

He pulled back and kissed her gently on the forehead. "You OK?"

She nodded, lying.

He frowned, realising. "You're not OK." He cast around looking for some sort of buoy to grab on to. "What would make this OK? What do you want to do?"

It was at that point that she kissed him.

"You hear the radio this morning?" asked Rake.

The pub needed a clean. Most times of year, tobacco was the main decoration. The ash and dust got into the dark red seats and mixed with the mud on the floor. The air was thick with it and the lights low. To remind punters of the season, the owners had put up tinsel—it looked like it had come from the 70's and resembled the stuff his parents had at home. Coloured foil, stuck together so that it squashed down neatly to be stored in the attic over the year, and then you pulled it out to long sparkly shapes that draped across the room, dropping down in places like chandeliers. It smelt strange, somehow metallic, tinny and electric, as if it remembered how it was made.

"Why, what happened?" asked Stacie.

Rake shrugged. "They called up some guy on a prank call and—"

"Hey, Rake!" Cezek sat next to him, something Cezek usually avoided as it made him look even shorter. "You shoulda been here last week. I found the best girl for you!"

"What?"

"She was tall, thin, gothic and a right minger. She looked like a man in drag!" Cezek laughed. "Totally your type. I got her number for you, and told her how nice you are, so you can meet her!" Cezek handed him a number on the scrap of paper. Rake glanced down. It was an 08900 number, one of those forty-pence-a-minute numbers, and Rake guessed that were he to ring it he'd find himself chatting to some escort agency that had been dumb enough to put a card in a phone box near Cezek's house. That or the dog-catchers.

"Fucker!" said Rake.

Cezek laughed. "Seriously, blood, I told her everything about you, she's desperate to meet you, she said something about having spare tickets to Suede's next gig."

"Lying cunt!"

Cezek laughed and then headed up to the bar. "I wouldn't go on a date with any girl Cezek finds you," said Stacie.

"Cezek didn't even talk to her," said Gary. "He just ripped the piss out of her from afar."

Rake crushed up the number. "Nice fucking cunt that he is."

"She might come in again," said Seth. "She looked lonely, like she was stood up. Probably the last thing she needed was Cezek."

"The last thing anyone needs is Cezek," muttered Rake. "Imagine the poor fuck who sees him as his last thing..." Everyone was staring at him in alarm.

The door bashed open and Helene strolled in. She went straight up to the bar and stood close to Cezek, perhaps trying to persuade him to buy her a drink, perhaps trying to get him in to bed with her. She was dressed up nice—short skirt, thick tights cos it was cold and she wasn't stupid, long black leather trench. On the top she had a corset top, laced up to within a millimetre of losing structural integrity and falling apart, and, because even dressed up in her best, cheap Woolwich Market fare she was sensible, she had a cardigan on under the coat for warmth. It was unbuttoned so Cezek could get the full view of her cleavage, which wasn't all that much as Helene was skinny. She'd even lost her glasses and gone for make-up, sort of vampy. Rake thought it looked quite good on her—it made her look older, more experienced. It was similar to the way Jane did her eyes.

Then he frowned, examining the table-top. He didn't notice that Helene and Cezek had returned until Helene elbowed him by accident as she sat down. She was grinning at Cezek, making eyes at him in a way she thought was oh-so-subtle.

"Thanks for the drink, Cezek," she said, sort of breathily like she was trying to be sexy. It was obscene watching her.

"Hah! I spiked it, you sure you want to drink it?"

She chewed on her lip, eating her pinkish lipstick. "You wouldn't, why would you do that?"

Cezek laughed. Helene sniffed her drink.

"It's fucking E, you'll be huggy and smiley in no time at all."

She sniffed her malibu and lemonade and then offered it to Seth.

"There's nothing in it," he said.

31

"You sure?"

"I didn't sell him any." He picked up the drink, looked at the top, took a sip. "It's fine," said Seth, shaking his head.

She frowned, still unsure, and then took a cautious sip of her drink.

"It's cyanide," said Cezek. Seth sighed.

She stared at Cezek and he laughed too loudly.

"Ah, Helene, you don't believe me, do you? You know I would never do anything to hurt you."

She smiled, sappily.

"I'd never spike your drink." He winked at everyone around the table to include them in the joke.

"Sorry."

Cezek nodded, suddenly serious now. "I can't believe that you would think I would do something so horrible."

She was chewing on her lip like it was the rind of a pork chop that she had to eat to get desert.

"I'm your friend, always looking out for you, and this is what you think of me?"

"I'm sorry, Cezek, you know I didn't mean it."

He gave her that predatory stare that she always seemed to misread for romantic passion. She smiled. Rake took a sip of his drink and wondered what the hell Helene saw in Cezek.

"You bring any green?" Cezek asked Seth suddenly. Helene was left staring at the back of his head, wondering where her great romantic make-up scene had gone.

Seth nodded. "You want it now?"

"Yeah, let's move over there..."

They all got up, bags and coats and everything, and went and sat in the booth by the window. It was cold, because Cezek cranked the window open slightly, damp and dark. The owners didn't really give a fuck about the bar. The bartender was a fat and depressed man. No one knew if he knew that they smoked weed in the pub and ignored it or whether they got away with it because he paid so little attention. Still, they kept up the pretence of hiding it.

Seth got out the rolling mat. For a guy he had long fingernails—seriously, each one was about a centimetre and a half long. Once he had managed to extract Rake's telephone card from a payphone just by poking his fingernails in and slipping it out. Seth was a goth and no one could not know that. Other than the freakily long nails, he had dyed his long, straight hair jet black, wore black eyeliner and loved his New Rocks. He added to it by looking sallow and unfed, mostly because he was. His mum was a drug dealer. He had mentioned watching her weighing cocaine out when he was a kid. Who knew if that was true. The way he talked about it though, with a sense of finality, of reality, convinced Rake. The guy informed rather than boasted.

And he always had a lot of shit on him. You name it, he had it: E's, coke, barbiturates, ketamine, whatever. And he knew how to mix it up as well—what went with what, what made a good night out rather than a trip to the hospital. It was a shame Cezek didn't listen to him.

As the bartender had fucked off to the kitchen, Seth laid out the rolling mat on the table. He laid some giant Rizlas out into a set-square shape and stuck them together.

"Rake, you got some baccy?" Seth asked.

Rake frowned. "Hardly any, ask Helene."

She scowled at him. "C'mon, I only got two left," she said, waving her menthol Marlborough Lights at Rake.

This was a losing move as Cezek nicked the box from her and grinned.

"These'll do," he said.

"Come on, give 'em back! That's all I got."

"You can buy more."

"C'mon, it's like four-fucking-fifty a pack in here."

"You can go to the corner shop."

"It's cold out there. And what if he won't sell it to me, will you buy them for me?"

Cezek laughed. "Just show him your flat chest in that corset, you'll get anything."

Helene blushed and reached for the ciggies and Cezek moved them slightly out of reach and grinned at her. "C'mon, Helene, share."

With a good stretch, the ciggies were well within her reach, but she didn't grab for them.

"Ceeeezeeeeek! Don't nick my smokes! Take Rake's, he doesn't even pay for his, just nicks them from his old man."

"Nah, I've nicked yours. And anyway, you've not paid for the green."

"Ceeeezeeeek!" Weirdly, she still didn't go for her cigarettes. Rake realised that she had given up and was just dicking around.

Cezek grinned and passed them to Seth, who took the ciggies without a word.

"Thanks, Helene," said Cezek, grinning at her.

She sighed and took a sip of her drink.

Seth rolled the cigarettes between his fingertips, dropping tobacco and sawdust onto the papers. Then out came the plastic baggies. They were the sort of thing you found tacky jewellery in in places like Woolwich Market. One bag was larger and had good-quality green in it, the leaves dried up like little dead spiders, all spiky legs and crispy. The other bag was a thick, sticky resin, the rough stuff—shish, as it was known, cos it smelt like shit. It only tasted as bad as burnt plastic.

"You putting that shit in?" asked Gary.

Seth nodded. "Makes the green go further."

"Fuck."

He crushed three spiders, dropping their dust in amongst the tobacco, then he held a chunk of shish between his finger and thumbnail and attacked it with Helene's lighter. As she'd been fucking with it, the flame must have burnt his fingers.

"You got fucking asbestos fingers," said Rake.

Seth shrugged, blowing on the rock, then crumbling it into the papers. "You get used to it."

His nails were yellowed, so maybe you did. He ripped the end of Rake's Rizla box and rolled it up to make the 'roach'.

"The best sort of paper for this, specially if you expect the Old Bill to be on the look out for torn Rizla boxes, is pages from the Bible." Seth's voice was flat, like he'd used up all the emotion he'd had earlier on in his life and he was now running on fumes. "Best type is one owned by someone that really believes, so the pages have been soaked in tears of religious fervour. You want their finger oils and sweat to have permeated the cover, so you want to nick one from a Jehovah's Witness or a market preacher, someone who's really gripped onto it like a fucking life belt." Seth didn't talk much, but when he did, everyone shut up and listened; the guy was a Beat poet in the 90s. "You use the cover for the roach and pages from Revelations with the best skunk you can find and that, my friends, is a fucking apocalyptic high." His laugh was high and reedy and Rake believed that the crazy fucker had actually done this.

"You are a complete fucking nutcase," said Cezek approvingly.

Seth's laugh ended abruptly and his face went back to matching the Easter Island heads. Then he expertly rolled the whole lot up, licking the papers and folding it round into a fat spliff.

"That'll fucking do you," muttered Seth, holding it out to Cezek. He then changed his mind and handed it to Helene with a watered-down smile. "As it was your baccy."

She grinned and took the spliff. It looked wrong on her. Helene was different from the rest of them, Rake mused. He wasn't sure what it was. Maybe that she was bright. Every day she rode two buses to a grammar school eight miles away—Plumstead Manor, where Stacie went, not being good enough for her. Helene had dreams, plans to get out of Plumstead, go to some fancy university somewhere and study whatever girls like her studied. And she did study. She read books and even went to the library through choice.

The thing was no one at her nice, middle-class grammar school liked her, so she still hung out with her old Plumstead Junior School friends.

Helene looked around the pub furtively, then lit the end of that fat spliff. She dragged on it as much as possible, as if it were, well, what it was: free, good-quality drugs. She coughed a little from the shish, pulled harder and then grinned, allowing the smoke to escape from her nostrils.

"Gimme that." Cezek grabbed it off her.

She grinned at him.

"This shit makes me so hard I could fuck all night," he said to her as he took a drag. And, sickeningly, she smiled even wider.

"Perhaps we'll test that out?" She tilted her head to the side and tried to raise one eyebrow. They both went up. All subtlety left her when Helene was high. Then she giggled.

"What the fuck is this?" Cezek was looking at his smoke. "Fucking menthol? Jeez, that's weird."

"It's good for you then," said Stacie, grabbing for the spliff.

Cezek waved the end at her. She jumped back.

"Stupid fucker!"

"Nah, this goes to my favourite female in the pub," he said, and grinned at Helene. She looked ecstatic. As he passed it over to her he dropped it on her knee, burning her.

"Gah!" She grabbed it up, flicking off a hot rock onto the floor. Her tights had melted and she had a small, round, tell-tale burn. "Fuck!" She grabbed an ice-cube out of her vodka and Coke and pressed it on her knee.

Cezek laughed and Rake wondered if the fucker had the coordination to do that on purpose. Helene still took a few deep drags on the spliff, in between swear words, all the while holding the ice-cube on her knee.

"You all right?" asked Rake. She nodded, took a deep drag, showing off that those lungs were well-used in choir practice, then handed the spliff to him.

"It's fine, but now my fucking knee's cold." Her voice sounded raspy from the shish. She put the ice-cube in the ashtray, where it melted, turning the cigarette butts into ships on a dust-covered lake, like some aftermath of a nuclear holocaust. Rake mused on that as he took some slow drags on the spliff. The stuff was fucking lethal and he wondered how Helene was able to cope with it. Then Stacie held out her hands for it and he passed it to her. She ought to take bigger puffs as she had the body mass to take it, unlike Helene, but Stacie smoked like ladies were supposed to sip at wine: small hesitant tastes.

Cezek was now trying to show his concern about Helene's knee by touching her thigh. He was trying to move his hand up her skirt and she was fighting him off, both happy at the interest and embarrassed. Whilst all this was going on, Seth had rolled himself a second spliff, no shish, and he was smoking it quietly. Despite the fact that Cezek was fighting with everyone for control of a spliff, no one tried to share Seth's. The guy didn't share.

There was no noise, but a blue light punctuated the scene, some sort of dot-dash-dash dot-dash-dash of an insane Morse code enthusiast. Seth dropped his spliff, clambered over Stacie and trod on Gary in his haste. He threw back the plate glass door at the back of the bar and was over the garden fence in a jump. For a weedy fucker, Seth could move. A policeman entering the bar gave chase and floundered at the fence. Second attempt, he got over.

The rest of them stared. Cezek passed the spliff to Helene, who, stupidly, took a puff, until a second police-man entered the bar and she dropped it in the ashtray, adding the Titanic to what was left of the iceberg.

It was fucking strange to see the Old Bill in Plumstead.

The landlord waddled over and pointed. "Look at that, officer!" He turned to them. "Haven't you fuckers seen the posters? No fucking drugs on the premises, I ain't losing my license over you morons."

That answered the question of whether or not the

landlord knew about it.

The copper sighed. His comrade returned, panting.

"So, who supplied it?"

They looked at each other.

"She did." Cezek was pointing at Helene. "She's the fucking coke lord of Plumstead." He laughed.

"Do you have coke on you, young lady?" asked the copper.

Helene started to sniff. "I... no..." She looked at Cezek in bewilderment. "I never even done coke and it wasn't mine!"

"Her baccy," said Cezek.

"Fucker!" whispered Gary.

"I... but it was your idea, and..."

Cezek grasped the front of Helene's corset and pulled her towards him. "You want me to lose my job, bitch?" he hissed.

She started gnawing at her lip again, and then she pushed Cezek away from her and stared at the coppers, "Uh... it was mine, but please don't arrest me, me mum would kill me!"

"Name?"

"It's mine," said Rake.

He felt as stunned as the everyone else looked, but he continued, "I bought it off some black guy up Woolwich Market and decided to share it. Don't know his name. All my fault. Helene didn't even have any."

No one could believe that. Her pupils were as big as shot glasses.

The cops looked bored. A second cop car arrived, providing further visual punctuation.

"OK, you lot, empty out your pockets."

They did, and Helene tipped out her bag. She was reading *Gone with the Wind*. No one had any drugs on them.

"Well? You gonna arrest them, officer?" asked the bartender.

The policeman sighed. "In the cars, all of you."

"And you're all fucking barred, got that? I don't want to see none of you round here again! Fucking idiots."

They all climbed into the cars. Helene was crying and begging the policemen not to tell her mum. One cop yawned. It was eight pm on a Thursday, a couple of hours until the pubs kicked out and the real crime kicked off.

The policemen questioned each of them about where they got the drugs. They all told a different and plausible story except for Cezek, who dobbed Seth in. Then, to meet their targets, the police gave each of them a verbal warning, filled in a form and told them to go. Only Rake was told confidentially by the copper to not be so fucking stupid in future.

When Rake left the police station everyone else had gone. He didn't bother asking the coppers for a lift home, and walked all the way up the huge fucking hill.

Dealing with the Devil

2008: Lehman Brothers, Canary Wharf

Cezek appeared in Rake's office. He looked cleaner—neat, in fact—in his look-at-me expensive Armani suit. He grinned.

"All right, mate," he said.

Rake sighed and cursed Tony for picking that stupid club last night.

"Nice office," Cezek added, looking around. "So this is what you did after your mum kicked you out."

"She didn't kick me out, I left."

"You never came back. I went and asked them about you."

Cezek had been to his house? "Why?"

"What do you mean, 'why'?"

"Yeah, why the fuck you care? I don't understand this."

Cezek shrugged. "I don't know why. We were mates, weren't we?"

"Were we? I'm not so fucking sure."

Cezek looked confused, and then laughed.

"You kept tabs on the others?" Rake tried to look casual, but he was watching Cezek intently.

"Well, you know, Stacie and Gary got fatter and fatter, then they got married, had kids and got even fatter." He shrugged. "They're fucking boring."

"Seth?"

Cezek laughed. "Arrested, bailed, arrested, bailed—you probably know him, he's still selling."

Rake laughed. "Not up here."

"Maybe not. He never did like the city."

Rake waited. Cezek didn't mention Helene.

"So, yeah, what can you promise me on my money?"

"I can't promise you anything, it's gambling."

"Hah hah. Yeah, but really."

"Really, it's gambling. Highly paid, fucking genteel gambling." Rake grinned. "And that's the friends' rate for you there, we don't tell most our clients that. We go on about our percentages, past achievement and how we've got our fingers on the fucking pulse of the world and make the sale before the fuckers even read the small print."

Cezek looked unsure. "Oh. You like it?"

Rake grinned. "I love it. I feel like a fucking king, and every time I pull off a big profit, I get a cut. Jeez, I am a long fucking way from Plumstead."

Cezek laughed. "Ain't we all."

Rake's smile left him. Cezek wasn't all that far from Plumstead. He was rich—in fact, he owned large swathes of it, cheap rentals, shit like that. And he had fancy properties in his portfolio as well. Rake had kept tabs on his old friend. He had been expecting the day when he would be called to the Old Bailey as a character witness on a murder charge.

"I want in."

"You want in? On what exactly?"

"I want in on this. I want some of those fucking percentages. My bank's taking me for a fucking ride, letting my money sit there, not doing nothing."

"Other than buying houses."

Cezek leaned forward. "You'll do for me?"

Rake paused. He wanted to Cezek to fuck off, explain exactly why he wanted the cunt to fuck off, but he paused. Cezek was worth a lot of money. And the stupid fuck hadn't even bothered to do anything with it. He was too fucking Plumstead to even spell investment. Rake could do a lot with that money—he could make it dance, make it sing, make it whore itself out on the street for a fat profit.

Rake smiled and put his hand out. "I'll take care of it."

Cezek grinned and shook his hand.

They hammered out the details, or rather, Rake got all the information he needed. Then just as Rake's mind was churning over the deals he could be making with it, should be making—the stock he should buy, the quick buck, the long steal—just as his head was full of figures, percentages and the much more lauded, less rational, instinct for what the market felt, Cezek asked: "You heard anything from Helene?"

Rake stared at him.

Cezek smiled. "I, er, lost contact with her, but I heard she went up town too."

Rake nodded slowly. "I don't know where she is. And I don't know that she'd want to see you."

Cezek frowned. "I wasn't going to visit... and anyway, of course she'd want to see me." He looked at him. "Wouldn't she?"

Rake was speechless.

"Course she would. Every fucking woman wants a

piece of me."

"Oh, you discovered sex finally, have you?"

Cezek laughed. "Don't be so fucking superior, I know more about women than Hugh Hefner."

Rake sighed.

"Well, I'd best fuck off then, see you soon."

"Bye." Rake watched him go and thought, his head on his hand, as he watched the red ticker-tape numbers blink by, millions being bought and sold, lost and won each second—he was losing time and he didn't even fucking care.

Helene...

Common People

1996: Plumstead Common

Rake and Helene were watching the city again. Rake looked up, squinting through the swift-sailed clouds to the night sky above. He couldn't see what was so special about stars. The light pollution made the sky behind the clouds look dark purple, the clouds muddy, the stars faint.

He looked down at the lights of the city, the constellations of the roads. These were their stars—they twinkled and sparkled and were even coloured. The planes above were their shooting stars, their comets, their portents of doom.

"You think a verbal warning's on my record somewhere?" said Helene. "Would I have to declare it on my UCAS form?"

Rake chuckled. "I doubt it."

"But... you have to declare a criminal record, do I have a criminal record now?" She whispered the last bit.

"A verbal warning is just that, a verbal warning. Did they tell you not to be so fucking stupid as well?"

"What?"

"Well, I got a 'don't be so fucking stupid' comment as well as a warning."

She shook her head. "I'm relieved. If it's verbal, it can't be a criminal record, cos records are written down, right?"

Rake nodded.

Helene pulled out her fags and offered him the packet. He took one, but refused her lighter and ended up having to offer her his as hers was running on fumes again.

"Thanks, Rake," said Helene, with enough import that he knew that she was talking about the night before and not the lighter.

Rake shrugged. "It wasn't fair you should take the rap."

She nodded. "Seth ran. Maybe we should've."

"He's got practice, I s'pose. And would you have been able to outrun the cops?"

Helene chuckled. "No fucking way."

They watched the stars of the earth singing to the mud of the sky.

"Howcomes I didn't see you on the walk back?"

"Cezek gave me a lift."

Rake stared at her. "You got in a car with that fucker?"

She nodded. "It was quite a walk home."

Rake knew. Plumstead police station was at the bottom of the hill. The grass where they were sitting was at the top. It was a long fucking walk. For people who had never seen mountains, it was the nearest thing they knew. Rake had enjoyed careening down it on a bike, avoiding the traffic and hoping for the best. He'd once chased the fucker who'd stolen his bike down there—there was no way in hell he would ever catch him, not over that terrain where the bike had the advantage, but he had still run and run, unable to stop without breaking an ankle. The guy had been far, far away, but Rake had still chased him onto an estate. Once there, in the unknown parkour territory, he'd lost the fucker.

"He was stoned," said Rake. "Don't get in the car with him when he's stoned."

She shrugged. "He drove slow."

No shit. When you were stoned everything seemed faster than it was. Something to do with your internal time running faster as your mind tried to process the fucking drugs.

"What d'ja mum say when you got in?"

"Ah, she was mega mad. I spun some lie about kipping at Stacie's and she believed it, but I was late to school."

Rake rewound and replayed her answer. "You didn't go home last night."

She shook her head, chewing on her lip.

"You fuck him then?"

"No."

Rake waited.

"I stayed over, in his room."

Rake raised his eyebrows. "Oh? And you didn't fuck him? What, you realised he's an arse like I keep telling you?"

She grinned and hit him on the arm, and then looked troubled.

"No... I mean I wanted to, and I thought that he did, but..."

"But what?"

"But... I don't know, I don't understand. I know he fancies me, right? He wouldn't touch me up in the pub if he didn't."

Rake rolled his eyes.

"And we're mates, so isn't that enough? I mean, to start a relationship, cos he likes me and he knows me and we get on. His mother thinks we're dating, she keeps making hints about it—"

"Oh, so you must be, then."

"I don't know! Sometimes, like when we're alone specially, he acts like he loves me."

Rake stared at her. "He ever say that?"

She shook her head. "He's kinda hinted, you know? But then, there we are, and his mother's cool with me staying over, you know, and she bought him a double bed and everything, but..."

"But he just rolled over and went to sleep? He kick you in the night? I could see him doing that and pretending to be asleep."

She started chewing on her lip again. "I slept on the floor."

"What?"

"I slept on the floor, in a sleeping bag."

"You gotta be kidding me."

She nodded.

"And he has a double bed?"

"Well, he said he needs his room, you know, and apparently I breathe too loud."

"You snore?"

She shook her head. Of course not—she had fine bone structure and a neat little nose. That was, so she had once told him, why she could sing well. "He snores. Like a hoover."

Rake nodded.

"But is it me? Why does he seem so interested and then just go so cold like that? He likes me, he must do, but then..."

"Cos he's an arsehole. Just move on, find yourself a nice guy."

She shook her head. "I can't. Nice guys seem to like me, but... I think I love him."

"Cezek?"

She nodded.

"You don't love Cezek. You're not that stupid."

"I do. Or I think I might do. Y'know?"

Rake shook his head. "I don't get it, I just don't. He's an arse, he treats you like utter crap, he burnt you—"

"That was an accident."

"Like hell, and then he tried to get you to take the rap for the drugs—"

"But what about his job?"

"What about your career? Don't you think the world needs another microbiologist more than it needs another fucking estate agent?"

"Cytologist," she muttered.

"Whatever. And you know he spiked your drink."

"What? He said he didn't, Seth said he didn't, and you..."

"Not yesterday, another day."

"When? Why?"

"When? Well..."

"Well? When?"

"Uh, last Friday."

She frowned. "Oh, God, I was ill that night..." She looked at him, far more clear-eyed than she had been the other night. "I ended up rushing home straight after that. I was soooooooo sick, I ended up taking the day off work. Me mum thought I had food poisoning."

"What the fuck did he give you?" Rake assumed it

would have been E or Rohypnol or something.

She shrugged. "Are you sure? I just can't believe he would do that." She pulled on her cigarette. "I'm sure he wouldn't do that."

A Bad Idea

2008: Rake's Penthouse, Poplar

It was actually not as hard as he had thought to call her after years. Her mum remembered him and was more than happy to give out her mobile number after a half-hour chat about what he was up to these days and how his mother was doing. And then he looked at the number in his phone, mused about why he was calling her. Just what the fuck did he hope to achieve by it? Then, just as he was about to give up, his thumb punched the call button and then it was ringing, the sound falling into a well of silence.

Then she answered. "Hello?"

"Uh... Hi, Helene."

"Hi."

There was nothing but the slight crackle of the line.

"Who is this?"

"Oh, oh, yeah, it's Rake. How are you?"

"Who?"

"Rake? Sebastian Rake. Y'know—"

"Rake! Oh, my God, I thought it was you, but—how are you?"

"I'm fine."

"Good, good..."

"So, er, I was wondering, are you free for dinner?"

"Dinner... let me see, I can fit you in this Tuesday at nine, is that too late?"

"Uh, no, I can—I guess I can get cover..."

"Oh, you working? We could do later."

"Say ten-thirty?"

"Sure, can we meet centralish?"

"Yeah, Leicester Square OK?"

"Sure."

Rake was there early. When Helene wandered in, Rake was quixotic, both impressed and disappointed. She was wearing the uniform of a female of his tribe: a deep red business suit. Hers came with a knee-length skirt and Jimmy Choos and all the berries: statement Mulberry handbag, glossy berry pout and even a Blackberry held to her ear. She paused at the door, talking, then spied him and smiled. Walking over slowly, texting now, she sat, mouthed 'sorry', finished the text and put the damned thing in her bag.

Then she looked at him properly. Rake glanced around the restaurant to let her feel that her looking was unobserved. It was a pricey place, full of people with money, and, best of all, it served food and drink until late into the night without ever quite getting that seedy club atmosphere or clientele. The place had lots of private little alcoves. The mirrors were there to bely that privacy.

In the mirror they matched, he in his smart suit, fresh from the office, and her in hers.

"Hi, Rake," she said when he glanced back. The large triple diamond and platinum engagement ring glinted when she moved her hand.

"Hi."

A waiter appeared. He ordered sushi, she some sort of grilled fish salad, then a bottle of the most expensive white wine and some fizzy mineral water.

"You're not a biologist, are you?" Rake asked.

She laughed, swinging her head so her perfectly coiffed straight statement-highlighted hair caught the light like an antique tin helmet. "Do I look like a biologist?"

He shook his head.

"So how are you, Rake?"

"Fine."

She nodded. Then laughed. "God, this is awkward, I didn't expect it to be awkward."

He nodded.

"Been a long time."

He nodded.

She sighed. "God, I sound like a talking cliché. Say something, Rake, to stop me from gabbing on."

"What do you do?"

"Consultancy. Biggest racket around, really."

He laughed. "You've obviously not been around the City lately."

"Have you? You look like you've done well for yourself."

Rake grinned. "Yeah, I'm an investment banker."

She raised her eyebrows, calculating his probable yearly salary. "Ahhh."

"And you, why consultancy? Why not microbiology?"

"Cytology—the study of cells. Human cells, y'know,

cancer and all that. Not microbiology." She grinned. "I never could be bothered with bacteria; what's the point? Mankind discovered bleach."

He nodded. "And now?"

"And now? Now I walk into offices, tell people what they already know, normally what their employees know, and get paid shitloads for it." She grinned. "Y'know, when I left uni and got this gig, I earnt two times more than my mum in the first year and I don't have anyone else to support."

"I thought you were going to be a scientist. Wasn't that your dream?"

She frowned. "Rake, it was a lot of money. I could have sat there, doing some fucking PhD, poor as shit—" The people on the next table looked over, shocked at the swearing. Helene had suggested the restaurant, and he supposed she moved in more genteel circles now. She flicked her eyes over to them and dropped her voice. "I wanted out of that. They offered me money for nothing really. A bit of bullshit here, a bit of business knowledge there, nothing at all." She leaned back and sighed off into the distance. "Yeah... I was tempted." She grinned.

"And now I earn shitloads. It's like Rich says. You know, he said the City was some endless shovelling of shit, but not shit, money. Just sloshing around the City from left to right and back again. You gotta be there to get your percentage. And corporations just want to spend it. The more they spend, the more they can get, the better their bottom line looks, y'know? And you gotta have money flowing in and out of your company. Hoarding it makes you look like you're not growing." She sighed and took a gulp of the white wine. Helene was no connoisseur.

"And at first, I was incensed when he told me that. I

remember, we were walking around the river by Battersea bridge, just chatting, kinda like you and I did when we were kids, and I thought, how is that fair? Why should people in the City get all the cash, y'know, and not teachers or scientists? He said, cos they're the ones that are making it, y'know, people who make the money get the biggest share, it's only fair."

Helene stuck her little feet out and examined the points of her shoes for a second and then grinned. "So I thought, why be a mug and starve my way through my PhD when I could have an amazing lifestyle, amazing shoes, more than I ever dreamed of as a kid."

"This Rich, is he your fiancé?"

She looked confused. "How'd you know about that?"

Rake pointed at the ring.

"Oh." She looked troubled.

"When you getting married?"

She shrugged. "Y'know, it's so hard to make space in our diaries. Rich is a consultant too, you see, very high-powered, we both travel a lot and I simply don't have time to organise a wedding." She fiddled with the stem of her glass. "Still, we got plenty of time, no rush."

Their food turned up. Helene flaked her salmon into bits and chased them around the vegetables with a fork.

"What about you?" she asked.

"What?"

"What are you doing? I thought you wanted to be an actor."

Rake chuckled. "Yeah, I did. I did a few auditions but, y'know, I love my job."

She nodded.

"The sheer power... it's like I'm the king of the world, or rather finance. I'm there, quick as a kingfisher, grabbing the stocks and selling at just the right point—before the meal is too cooked, you know, just at the point where the fish flakes from the bone."

He looked at Helene's salad. She wasn't eating it. She looked good though. She'd filled out from when she'd been a teenager. The high cheekbones still suited her. She was still petite, but less of a stick than she had been.

Rake stopped checking her out when he realised that he was checking her out.

He grinned, speared a shrimp with his chopstick and wolfed it down. "I love my job," he added as a conclusion on the whole thing.

She nodded. "Sounds more like the sort of job Cezek would like," she muttered before finally eating a morsel of her salad.

Rake stared at her. "You, er, heard from him?"

She laughed. "Why the hell would I?"

He shrugged. "You know what he is now?"

She rolled her eyes. "My job is knowing who people are. Are you asking me if I know he's rich? I do. You think that would change my decision?"

Rake stared.

She frowned, then grinned. "No, that's not what you were asking about." She waggled her fork at him. "He's come to see you, hasn't he?"

"I bumped into him."

"Professionally?" Rake nodded. "I'm surprised."

"Why?"

"Why? You always acted like he was dangerous, like the devil incarnate, instead of what he is."

"And what is he?"

She sighed like a rockfall. "A very sad and lonely little boy." Rake just stared. "You were right, you know," she added. "If I'd ended up with him, well..." She shuddered and Rake wasn't a hundred percent sure whether it was put on or not. Then she smiled at him.

"Are you happy?" he asked.

The smile faded.

"People don't usually ask that," she said eventually. She put on another plastic smile. "It's not polite."

"Oh? Are we that distant that I have to be polite?"

"It's been over ten years, Rake."

"You haven't answered the question."

She shook her head. "Oh, for goodness' sake, of course I'm happy. Yeah, maybe there's some things I might change. I could be thinner, for one—"

"You look fantastic."

"Well, y'know, I do yoga and all that shit when I get the time."

He nodded.

She grinned. "I hardly ever get the time. I think it's coffee and cigarettes."

"Ah, you still smoke? You've not gone into the whole vegan, clean living thing?"

"As if. Only the yoga, and that's cos it's better than running."

"Yeah. You know..." He paused. "You could have called me."

"I didn't have your number."

Rake placed his hands palm down on the tablecloth. "C'mon, you were as capable of ringing up my mum as I was of ringing up yours."

She didn't look surprised and Rake figured her mum had told her, although she could have figured it out.

"What did you expect? You left."

"I escaped."

"What about me?"

"What about you? You were already on an escape trajectory, you were on your way out, you had things sorted."

She chuckled. "Escape trajectory. You sound like you're on *Star Trek*."

A waiter came over and poured more wine in the totally obvious way of someone trying to be unobtrusive. When he was out of range, they continued.

"What did you come here for, Rake?"

"I don't know."

She nodded to herself. "You're getting old."

"What the fuck? How am I old? I'm fucking twenty-nine!"

She grinned.

"I came to warn you."

"Warn me about what?"

"Cezek."

"Cezek?"

"Yes, he's... well, he found me. It was pure chance, but I got this feeling that, well, he's gonna seek us all out."

"Why?" She leaned forward and Rake had a good view of her cleavage.

"Why? I don't know. The stupid fuck. He was—how can I put this? I don't know. He's dangerous, Helene."

"You've said that before."

"I know. But he is."

"Why?" She was leaning further forward, in danger of knocking the glass on the floor with her elbow. Rake would have looked down her top but he was captured by her kohled and mascaraed eyes. "You always say that. Why? What haven't you told me?"

Rake just stared at her.

"Well?"

He smiled smoothly. "I don't know anything I haven't already told you."

She leant back, sighed, and then took a gulp of her wine. "You always protect him."

"That wine's expensive, why you gotta gulp it like that?"

She grinned. "I know it's fucking pricey and I glug it like cheap cider. I think that's fucking cool. And don't act like you're a connoisseur, you know as little as me." He chuckled. "So don't change the subject." She waved the glass at him and Rake realised that she was skating on the edge of pissed.

"You should eat your salad."

She shrugged.

"And I don't protect him. I never have. It's you I wanted to protect."

She dropped the glass.

The Out Plan

1996: Above a Curry House, Welling

"Why don't you just leave the fucker?" Rake was lying in Jane's bed, running his hands over her bare stomach.

"I thought we'd agreed no questions."

Rake frowned in perplexity. "But surely you must be able to see..."

Jane got up, pulled on her dressing gown and walked into the en suite.

Rake was left with a face full of pillow.

He padded over and knocked on the door. "Jane?"

"Just... leave, Seb."

He frowned. Then banged on the door. "Come on, come out."

"Just go away."

Bemused, he pulled on his clothes and walked into the main room. He called a goodbye and then opened and shut the main door. Then he sat quietly on the sofa.

As expected, about a minute after, Jane peeked around the door before she clocked him on the sofa.

"Oh," she said.

Rake grinned at his cleverness.

She sighed and she sat down next to him. "You really should, for yourself, just leave and don't come back."

Rake frowned then took her hands in his. They were so cold and fragile. "I don't want to leave, and when I do, I will come back." He kissed her hand and grinned.

She sighed. "I really should just tell you to go and not let you back in. I'm a terrible person." She shook her head, tears brimming in her eyes.

"Don't be stupid, of course you're not terrible. It's that fucker, he's making you think like this, you don't need to believe what a bully says."

She shook her head. "You don't understand, you really don't."

"So tell me, then. Make me understand."

She stood up then and looked at the clock. "Don't you have lectures?"

"What? What the hell?" Then he remembered that he'd told her he was a university student. *Do students really bother that much about lectures?* "Does that matter? This is more important."

She sighed. "I love him, that's all it is."

Rake ground his teeth. "You don't love him, don't be stupid. How could anyone love someone who hits a woman?"

She stiffened. "It's not like that. It's only when I upset him." She looked down. "And I'm so good at upsetting him."

"You couldn't upset anyone, you couldn't hurt a fly."

She shook her head. "No, I make him angry, that's all it is. When he's not angry, he's wonderful, you see?" She smiled weakly. "And that's why I'm not being fair to you. You do know that this is just sex, right?"

Rake nodded. What did he know about the difference

between just sex with a side-order of company compared to love and all the trimmings? All he knew was that he wanted to wrap Jane up in chiffon or something delicate and take her away somewhere safe, somewhere nice, somewhere where they could have a fucking picnic in the sun or whatever couples were supposed to do.

And he wanted to fucking kill Terry or whatever the fuck he was called.

"It's not fair on you if you don't understand that," persisted Jane.

"What about what's fair on you? You ever thought about that?"

She shrugged. "I'm a terrible person. You don't know. You don't believe me, but it's true. I don't deserve any better."

"Yes, you do. Ditch him. If he comes around here looking for trouble, I'll be here. I can move in to protect you."

She looked at him in alarm.

"Look, Seb…" She looked up at the clock and then smiled a fool's gold smile. "I'll think about it, but now, I really got to get on and you must already be late."

Rake sighed. "I'll see you tomorrow night," he said, then he kissed her.

She nodded vaguely.

———————————

"So then these kids, right, they were throwing things off the balcony—y'know, TVs, irons, shit like that." Stacie was speaking.

They had moved to another local pub. Rake didn't like this one so much. It was the one his old man drank in and he was worried that his old man's mates might report back on what he got up to. But this one was technically closer to his home and was called the *Who'da Thought It*. Rumour was that the pub sign had been a symbol of a man in a space rocket, then in 1961 they'd had to change that. Then it had been a man on the moon, that had lasted until 1969. Then they'd decided to just change it to a flying pig. About once a month some wit made some joke about soaring porcine stock and suggest they change the sign.

"But the kids, they'd lived their whole lives in that fucking tower block, they didn't even know that the things moving around below them was people."

"What did they they think they were?" asked Helene, her eyes wide.

Stacie shrugged. "I don't know, ants or summink. But all I know is that the pigs had cordoned the area off, cos some poor fucker'd had his head smashed in by a TV set."

Helene shuddered. "I hate this place," she muttered.

"That wasn't here, that was down the road," said Stacie.

"Still fucking Plumstead though, weren't it?"

She shrugged. "This shit happens everywhere."

"No, it really don't."

Stacie frowned. "Oh? Where don't it?"

Helene shrugged.

"Up at school perhaps? Do you think you're better than us, just cos you got into some stuck-up grammar school?" Stacie was drunk, and she tended to take a turn for the nasty when drunk, although usually it was Gary that got his ears split by her.

"No—"

"Course, none of them fuckers there know anything about real life, they're all babied with their orchestras and their dance lessons and their choirs..."

Helene frowned. "I never said it was better at school.

I hate school, you know."

Gary interjected. "So why are you staying on to do A-levels? You don't have to."

Helene rolled her eyes and took a sip of her rum and Coke. "Cos you need them to get into university, don't you?"

"Why bother? I can get you a job with me brother."

She sighed.

"The princess thinks she's too good to work," said Stacie.

"That's not it at all!" blasted Helene. "I just want out, that's all, out of Plumstead. I hate it here. Everything is shit! And yeah, I hate school too. I'm gonna go further than just the 51 route, y'know? I'm going up to London, away from the suburbs. I'm gonna live there."

"As a student? You'll end up kipping at your mum's and commuting."

"I ain't commuting, no fucking way. I've had more than enough of that to last a lifetime." Helene was in many ways the most well-travelled of them, because she had a part-time shop assistant job up central London. To the rest of them, London was distant, a place of family and school trips on special occasions. Bexleyheath and Woolwich had everything they needed.

"There's a better life out there," Helene scoffed. "Anything's better than Plumstead."

Stacie pulled her most superior face. "You're a dreamer."

"So what if I am?"

"It's crowded, London," said Seth. "You can't see the fucking pigs, there are some round every fucking corner, giving directions to lost tourists or some shit..."

Cezek laughed. "They wouldn't even notice you

amongst everyone else in London."

"You want to go there?" asked Seth.

Cezek shrugged. "Maybe... Not really. Why would I? I got everything I need right here." And for some reason he smirked at Helene. It was, Rake thought, a cheap-shot cupid's arrow. Helene looked troubled though, rather than impressed. Maybe she realised that going to London would take her away from Cezek. A damned good idea as far as Rake was concerned.

"What about you?" asked Stacie, leering at Rake "You want to fuck off up town and be all hoity-toity as well?"

"I didn't say I would go forever." Helene was looking desperately from Stacie to Cezek. "I'd just live up there. We could still meet up."

"Nah, once you're out, you're out, y'know? People change up town, get different, no longer Plumstead."

"I wouldn't."

"Yeah, you would. That's the whole fucking idea isn't it? You want out of Plumstead, surely you want Plumstead out of you."

Cezek started laughing. "I don't think Helene could fuck a whole postcode."

They all stared at him.

"Well? Rake?" asked Gary. "What do you think? Would you get a job up town?"

Rake shrugged. "I might move to Welling."

"Why Welling?"

"Is that where Lise lives?" asked Helene. Rake nodded.

"Lise? Who's Lise?" asked Cezek.

"Me girlfriend." Rake grinned widely.

"You got a girlfriend?" Cezek looked disturbed.

"Yeah." Rake frowned at Helene. "I thought you'da

told them, it's not like a big secret."

Cezek narrowed his eyes at Rake.

"I don't gossip," Helene said sniffily. Rake figured it was more that she was more concerned talking about herself or Cezek or the possibility of both together.

"That's nice," said Gary to Rake. "Maybe you could move in with her and get a job, stop scabbing beers off us."

"Who the fuck you think you are? Me old man?"

"Don't fucking swear at him, Rake," said Stacie.

"Do your parents know yet?" whispered Helene, as if his old man was in the pub. Which was just as well, as some of his mates were gabbing up at the bar.

"What? About Lise?"

She nodded. "And, y'know, getting kicked out of school."

Rake shrugged. "So anyway, yeah, I was talking to Lise about moving in together, y'know. Then I can do what I want."

"Yeah, fucking parents," said Cezek, "always stopping you from doing what you want to do."

Rake eyed Cezek and wondered if his mum had ever managed to stop him doing anything.

"Welling doesn't count as moving away," said Stacie, in a self-satisfied way. "Pretty much the same as round here, just Bexley borough." She frowned at Helene. "Just you that thinks you're better'n us."

Helene bashed the table. "That's not it. I just hate Plumstead. There's no life here, no warmth, nothing." She looked out over the bar, taking in Rake's dad's mates, and dropped her voice. "If we don't get out now, that'll be it. We'll be lifers, ending up the same as our parents. Fuck, we're already drinking in the same pub. How long before the guys all get a CIU club pass and it's not even semi-ironic any more, and we'll be the next generation, stuck here forever?" She shook her head. "The warning signs are there. I don't know why you can't see them."

"I don't know why you're so fucking rude," said Stacie. "You wouldn'ta even thought of leaving if Chad were still living here."

Helene stared at her.

"He had dreams, you know, big dreams..." Then Helene covered her mouth with her hand, got up and left the pub. Rake made to go after her, but, unexpectedly, he saw Seth get up. As Seth was closer to the door, Rake stayed for a moment to scowl at Stacie.

"What the fuck?" he asked.

Gary eyed him like a terrier, ready to defend his master. Although Gary was bigger and stronger than Rake, Rake didn't give a fuck: Gary hadn't even known Chad.

"What?" asked Stacie, her innocent expression tainted by guilt. She raised her eyebrows. "It's been over a year now, am I still supposed to treat Madame de Helene like the fucking Queen?"

"You're drunk, and you're stupid when you're drunk," said Rake. "Just leave her alone, OK? And for fuck's sake, don't mention Chad."

"Yeah, don't mention Chad," echoed Cezek. Rake stared at the fucker. It was the first time he'd spoken for a while.

Stacie dry-gulped and nodded. "I didn't say nothing, only..."

Rake got up and left her to her drunken excuses and went outside.

Helene was squatting Indian style, curled up into a little ball, her butt just off the floor. Her red coat was against the grimy wall and the ends of it were sitting in the mud, moss and street dust. She was staring at nothing, sort of looking down the street towards the common. Seth was standing over her like a shade. He was just watching her and smoking. She took a drag on a roll-up that Seth must have passed her as an attempt at comfort. Rake and Seth exchanged a glance as Rake squatted down in front of Helene.

"You all right?" he asked.

She moved her head then, looking from the common to him. "Yeah." She blinked hard a few times, then took a deep drag of the rollie. "No," she finally admitted. "He did have dreams, you know? He wasn't going to stay around Plumstead forever. He was gonna get out, y'know, get on the up and up, end up somewhere good." There was an empty pause. "You know it's his birthday next week? He woulda been eighteen."

"Yeah, I knew that," said Seth. She looked at him and nodded.

She shook her head. "Poor fucker," she said, and then started crying.

Rake looked at Seth in alarm. Seth put his hand out awkwardly to put it on Helene's shoulder, but stopped short and stared at Rake in panic.

Helene shook her head, blinking away tears. She dragged on the rollie. It had gone out, as the fucking things usually did. Rake provided a light, happy to have something to do to help.

She took a deep drag. "I'm going home." Another drag. "I just gotta go in an' get me things..." She didn't look happy at the prospect. The door banged shut and Seth had gone. Rake was even more surprised when Seth returned a moment later with Helene's bag and purse. As a general rule, the guy didn't put himself out for people.

"Thanks," said Helene. She shook her head. "I'm sorry to be such a downer."

"Chad would want you to leave," said Seth.

She stared at him. "What? The pub?"

"No, Plumstead, if that's what would make you happy. He would..."

Helene nodded, smiling through her tears. "Don't worry. I am going to leave this shithole and I am going to be happy."

Response

2008: Lehman Brothers, Canary Wharf

Rake knew it had been a bad idea to take Cezek's money. It was always a bad idea to make a Faustian bargain. The cunt was back in his office two days after making the arrangements. He wanted to know the ins and outs of every deal, he wanted to hear Rake talk through what he was going to do and why, and the cunt was too fucking ignorant to know that was not the way it worked. You were supposed to choose from the options you were presented with, not take it as a chance for a cheap MBA and then make a big deal about how you were making the decisions.

"Right, mate, so we'll meet next week," said Cezek.

"Next week?" *What the fuck?* "I won't have anything I need to ask you by next week. The idea is that you leave the money where it is for a little while." *Why the fuck was he explaining this shit? Wasn't it obvious? If Cezek didn't fucking know then why the fuck didn't Cezek just leave the money with Rake and fuck off and buy himself another slummy ex-council flat?* "I'll call you in a month."

Cezek grinned. "Ah, but—"

Rake's Blackberry was vibrating in his pocket. Normally he would have ignored it, maybe glanced at the number, but he'd never answer it in front of a client.

It was a number he didn't know.

"Hello?" said Rake to the phone, looking at Cezek.

"Fucking five mil of my money not enough to hold your attention?"

"Hi, Rake." It was Helene. "I know you're busy, but I was thinking of further diversification of my investments. I've got nothing in media, you see." She was talking in fast quick-fire speech. *Was she nervous or was that how she talked at work?* "Perhaps we could meet one evening this week? Say Friday, over dinner again."

"Dinner?" Rake was looking at Cezek and moved away a bit, bending low and twisting, crushing the phone to his ear in hope that Cezek wouldn't hear who he was talking to.

"Yes. It's more friendly than a business meeting, wouldn't you say?"

He raised his eyebrows.

"And as this is a personal investment for me, I should do it outside of working hours."

He walked away from Cezek. "Look, I was planning to go to the Old Vic that night, I've got a box there—"

"Oh—"

"Would you like to come along? We can get dinner beforehand, and we'll have plenty of time to discuss business." Then he looked at Cezek. *Do I really want more business from old friends?*

"Ah, I see, sure."

"Meet me at Massimo's beforehand, it's on Northumberland Avenue."

"Sure, see you then."

She hung up and he wondered what she had been in

the middle of doing.

"Fucking hell, you just gonna stand there and stare at your phone all day?"

Rake smiled. "I can't be ahead of the curve if I don't take business calls."

Cezek laughed. "You looked more like you were chatting up some old whore."

"She's not a whore!" The vehemence of his comment took them both by surprise.

Cezek grinned. "Ah, tetchy, I see. Women, they're not worth the effort. Fuck everything up. It's good to have a couple around, but you gotta be careful. They love nothing more than leading you around by the balls, so you gotta not give them a fucking inch, cos they'll take it all and then expect you to say thank you or some shit."

"Cezek, I would not come to you for relationship advice. In fact, I'd go further—I could bloody well do without it, all right?"

Cezek laughed. "There's no point telling you anything. Your balls are your brain, and women have been leading you around by them your whole fucking life! You'd not know what to do if you managed to get out from under."

Magnolia Shirt

1996: Above a Curry House, Welling

Another hard day of doing nothing lay behind him. Rake had almost given it away to his mum that morning as he'd forgotten that Wednesday morning was double Drama, not double English. He was feeling pretty damn good for getting away with it for so long. As long as he wasn't in when his mum came home, she assumed he was at school, and, as sixth formers didn't have to wear uniform, he didn't look too out of place wandering around Woolwich. The only problem was the lack of money. All he had was school dinner money—he ate what he found at home—and his pay from stacking shelves at the Co-op was almost nothing. They didn't have any more hours available for him and, to be honest, at that point he'd stopped looking for work.

He had more important things to do during the evenings now.

He arrived at Jane's at about four pm. She let him in as soon as she heard his voice over the intercom and when he got upstairs he understood why. She and the flat were in a state—things had been trashed again, some of her plant pots were smashed and the fucker'd put some-thing through the TV. Worse was Jane. She grabbed him and started sobbing. She had black eyes and a swollen bruised nose. There were bruises and cuts on her upper arms.

"What the fuck happened?" asked Rake.

She shook her head, sobbing. "He came over, drunk... I don't know, I smashed a mug, and..." She put her head on him. "I didn't mean to, I'm just so clumsy sometimes, I can't do nothing quietly..."

"He did all this? For that?"

"He said he was tired from work, and he went on about what I spent money on." She shook her head. "But I bought those ornaments with my dole money, not his..."

Rake clenched his fist. "I am going to kill that fucker," he said.

She grasped hold of him again. "An' he says it's over. I didn't mean to upset him, it's not on purpose, I don't understand why..." She shook her head and wibbled on about china ornaments and tea-cups for a while. Rake just held her. Then when her sobs turned to whimpers he tipped her head back and kissed her.

"We'll sort this, OK? And if that fucker comes back, I'll fucking kill him."

She sniffed a few times and nodded. "He ain't coming back this time."

Rake stroked her hair. "Good. That's a good thing, isn't it?"

She nodded. "I hope I never see him again! I wouldn't ever let him near me again." She wrapped her arms around Rake. "You can come over whenever you want to now. You wanted to move in?"

Rake grinned. He was moving out of home that afternoon!

"Well"—she smiled shakily—"if you still want to..."

"Yeah. Sure. This evening, I'll tell them."

"Who?"

Rake almost said 'my parents'. "Me flatmates. I'll tell them I'm moving out." He grinned. "Not a problem."

She smiled back and unaccountably started crying again.

"Hey, hey, no need to cry, nothing to cry about at all, OK?" He pulled her close. She grimaced as he squeezed on her bruised arms. "Shit, sorry, sorry. It'll all be OK, Jane, everything will be OK."

Then he was kissing her gently. Everything was gentle. He was disgusted at the bruises—there were more—but he tried not to show that. He touched her very carefully, running his hands over the bits that weren't bruised. He treated her like the finest porcelain, as if the merest pressure from his hands would break her.

She started crying again, soundlessly. And then he was whispering, "I love you, Jane, I love you." And then she was crying and smiling and he wasn't even sure why. And then they were pulling off each other's clothes. And then they were fucking, right there on the carpet, next to the broken glass and ceramic shards.

And then the intercom buzzed. "Jane, you in?"

She pushed Rake off her. "It's Terry!"

Rake kissed her. "So?"

She hit him in the shoulder. "No, stop, it's Terry! He's here!"

And Rake remembered who the fuck Terry was. He was up like a shot and pulling his trousers on.

"Jane? Look, I know you're there. Let me in so I don't freeze me fucking balls off!"

"It'll be OK," said Rake. "Let him in."

"What are you going to do?"

Rake smiled. "Don't worry about that, you can hide in the bedroom."

"But..." She sniffed and waved a thin fist at him. "You tell him. Tell him to leave me alone!" Rake nodded.

Jane pressed the intercom button. "What the fuck you doing here?"

"What the fuck am I doing here? What the fuck do you think?"

"What about work?"

"Fuck's sake, woman, you think I don't know me own business? Foreman reckons those Irish bastards have planted another bomb, and I don't get paid for that shit, so don't you fucking start!"

"I want you to leave. Leave me alone. Fuck off. I don't want to see you no more!"

"What the fuck?" Rake heard that from the window. "Look, Jane, if this is about last night, I'm sorry, OK? I didn't mean to hurt you. You know how I feel about you. So come on, let me in, and we'll talk about it, OK?"

Jane was sniffing. Rake put his arms around her tenderly. She stiffened.

"Let him in, I'll deal with this." He kissed her on the temple. "It'll be OK."

"Who was that?" asked Terry.

Jane looked at Rake. "Please, just make him leave."

Rake nodded. She turned and walked into the bedroom.

Rake pressed the buzzer for the door and looked back to see Jane, now dressed in her dressing gown, peering round the bedroom door. "You might not want to watch this," he said.

She didn't close the door.

Someone hit the front door with a crash, the lock gave way, screws giving up, and the door shuddered open and Terry was there. He was a large, muscular man. He looked like what he was—a builder used to hefting bricks around all day.

Rake didn't know what he had expected Terry to do, but it wasn't what he did. Terry just stood in the door frame and looked from Rake to Jane for a few moments.

"Leave, OK?" said Rake. "She doesn't want anything to do with you anymore."

Terry laughed. "I fucking knew it, I did! You've got yourself a fancy piece! You fucking whore."

"Don't talk to her like that!" Rake moved in front of the door to the bedroom, his hands fisted and ready to fight. "Don't you dare!"

Terry laughed. "And what the fuck are you supposed to be? Fucking Clint Eastwood? Are you even old enough to shave? Run along back home to Mummy, you cunt."

"I ain't leaving. I live here now."

"Oh, you do, do you?"

"Yeah, and just fucking leave, OK? And don't think you're coming back here to threaten Jane."

This was it, if Rake was going to kill the fucker now was the time.

He glanced around for a weapon, wondering why he hadn't thought to find something before, and then glanced at Jane. He didn't want her to see this, but she was just staring at Terry.

Then Rake's head rang like a bell from Terry's meaty fist hitting his chin.

And then Rake didn't care who was watching.

He punched Terry back, feeling his fist driving into

the guy's nose, then Rake was pounding on Terry's chest. Maybe Terry was too used to people who didn't hit back as he seemed stunned by this and took a couple of blows.

Then Terry was fighting back. Terry was the bigger, stronger, more experienced fighter. Rake fought, but took far more than he gave. Then he felt himself being lifted by his belt and slammed up against the wall. He tasted blood from where his teeth crashed down on his tongue and then he was out the flat, dragged to the stairs then thrown like a scaffolding pole. He hit a ladder and some paint pots on the way down.

"Come back here again, and I'll fucking kill you!" shouted Terry.

Jane screamed and then the door slammed. Rake lay dazed for a moment. Then he pulled himself up. Magnolia paint was all that was covering his skinny, bloodied chest.

He looked up at the flat door. It was quiet. The fucker could be killing Jane for all he knew and there was nothing he could do about it.

The door opened momentarily and his coat sailed down the stairs and landed at his feet.

Birthday

1996: Plumstead Common

Rake was walking back. It was a dark night and a cold fucking one. The cold air didn't help his injuries, but the bus had sailed straight past him. He couldn't blame the driver—bus drivers had to clean the seats at the end of their shifts.

Rake wasn't dead though, and that fucker Terry soon would be.

He did his coat up to hide the blood and tried to clean his face up as much as possible. He walked though, knowing only a miracle of bus timetabling would mean that the next bus would get to him before he got home.

He was walking around the common when he happened to glance down into the dip. It was dark there, but only as dark as it ever got in Plumstead. The heavy clouds reflected the sodium lights and he could make out a figure standing motionless by the lake. He paused.

"Fuuuuuck!" Rake whispered. He looked around himself and then even checked his heartbeat. Yeah, he was alive and not in some spiritual realm or some shit. "Fuck, fuck, fuck..."

Birthday

What the fuck would he say to Chad?

Rake took a deep breath and headed down the dip. His trainers slipped in the dirt. When he was halfway down he recognised her.

He stopped at the bottom. "Helene?" he whispered.

She turned her head a little to the side, acknowledging his presence.

"What are you doing?"

"It's his birthday today. I was going to come earlier, but I couldn't and... I..."

Rake walked round her and saw that she had a bunch of white roses in her hands.

"Most people go to graves," he said.

She shrugged. "It was here he died, innit? Why put flowers anywhere else?"

"Oh."

"I still don't get it. It's not even that deep here. I know he couldn't swim, but he's not stupid..."

"He, er... was on skunk."

"Yeah? Well, why'd he go into the lake? When I'm stoned I don't fucking decide to go for a fucking swim."

Rake said nothing.

"Look, would you come with me?"

"Where?"

She pointed at the lake. "I want to leave them there, but..."

He looked at her, then he looked at the lake. She was right, it wasn't deep at all. Really it was two ponds, connected by a dam and a small island. It was about as deep as his shoulders at that point. It was a place they would play as kids—they weren't supposed to, of course, that's why there was the fence there, but someone had pulled the fence apart a bit and children could squeeze through.

his hand, feeling sick.

"Helene, it's OK," he said after a while. "It's OK. You didn't kill him."

"I know, I know that, but I feel so awful. He deserved better, but we were going to break up, but he didn't know that, no one knew that and..."

"It's still OK. You didn't have to love him. You made him happy, you know? And that's enough, OK? No one said you had to love him."

"But I was faking it at his funeral. Everyone was so nice, so careful with me, how could I tell them?"

"You didn't need to tell them anything. Even if you'd broken up with him beforehand, you would still have been upset, and everyone would still have been nice to you, you see? Even if you didn't love him in the end, you were there for him for years..."

"I... guess so. I just... It feels like I should have loved him more. Y'know? He deserved that."

Rake said nothing.

She looked down at the dark water. "A horrible way to die," she muttered. "You think he felt it? You think it was awful?"

Chad, thrashing around, kicking, splashing, Rake wading into the water trying to reach him, Seth somewhere behind, Chad's eyes rolling, bulging so Rake could see the whites of his eyes.

"No. The brain cuts off, lack of oxygen, he didn't feel nothing."

She nodded.

She let the flowers go. They drifted on the water, not really going anywhere. One spun around gently on an eddy current.

"I'm sorry, Chad," she whispered.

As if she'd been released from a spell, she turned and almost ran, not looking back once. Rake worried that she would tumble into the water herself. But she was through the fence in a moment and then she moved, purposefully up the path, under the trees. He followed her as quick as he could without risking a soaking and saw her standing under the first streetlight. As he walked up he could see she was staring at a small bit of blood on her white scarf, presumably from where she'd squashed through the fence.

"Rake, what—" Then she looked up and, he was pretty sure, took him in for the first time. "Fuck, Rake, what happened to your face? You're bleeding!"

"Ah, it's nothing."

"Nothing? Shit, you're really hurt! What happened?"

"Just..." He looked at his hand, his bloodied knuckles... *Am I just as bad as Cezek?* "Nothing."

"Shit! Come on, come back to mine, we'll sort you out."

"It's fine."

He was fucking cold, and Helene's house was only a minute's walk from the common...

"Come on, you're not walking all the way home like that. Let's sort you out."

Friday Night Date

2008: Massimo's, Westminster

Another fancy restaurant. Shining glasses, shiny cutlery, mirrors to reflect the sparkling little spotlights in the ceiling. Clean white linen, lowered voices other than the odd laugh ringing out. Rake waited. Then Helene cut through the crowd. He assumed that she had come from work. She was wearing one of those shift dress things, wool, expensive—probably fucking Prada—Jimmy Choos with those ridiculous points, another statement bag, this one with enough metal on it to be used as an offensive weapon, gold earrings, necklace, diamond bracelet.

She sat opposite him and smiled. "You're early again. You were usually late when we were younger."

"The markets don't wait."

"Right."

There was an awkward pause. They ordered avocado salad and chicken pasta.

Helene smiled, unsure. "I looked you up."

He nodded, expecting that, then poured out the wine. He was careful to only pour her half a glass.

"And I thought to myself, I don't have anything at all

in media, so would you mind investing a little for me?"

"For you, Helene, anything." She narrowed her eyes at him. "How much?" he asked, more to steer the conversation back into safe waters rather than because he needed to know.

"I was thinking thirty grand."

He looked at her with sympathy.

"Jeez, Rake, that's not all of it."

He grinned, relieved. "Oh, good. I thought consultants were paid better than that."

She rolled her eyes. "I'm not an idiot, I've split my money around."

"Where?"

"Well, y'know, I've mostly gone for safe investments—property, ICESAVE, Enron—I got some Korean bonds as well which are doing great at the moment." She grinned. "You're getting my danger money."

He laughed. "It's not dangerous."

She gestured at him with the glass. "Where do you put your bonuses then?"

He grinned. "Exactly where my mouth is. I manage most of my investments. All in media, film companies, music, that sort of thing."

She raised her eyebrows. "You didn't even think to diversify at all?"

"Pur-lease. I am not a moron. Tank's got some in construction, Danny-boy's got some in tech." He shrugged. "But believe me, I know my stuff and I am the person I trust most with it." She nodded. He smiled and leaned forward. "So any questions you want to ask?"

"What have you been up to these twelve years?"

He frowned. "I meant about the investments."

"Oh." She airily tossed her head. "No, it's fine, you

just do what you want to."

"I'll just roll it in with Cezek's then, save on the transaction fees."

"I'd rather you didn't."

"Why?"

"It seems kinda... obscene..."

"What?"

She shrugged. "I don't know, you'll think I'm nuts. Just, I'd rather you didn't."

"Oh." He frowned. "It's just money, Helene, it isn't him."

She looked perplexed. "But it kinda is, in some way, it's his money, made by him... I..." She shook her head. "No, it doesn't make any rational sense at all, does it?"

He smiled. "It's cool. I'll roll it in with mine then." He raised his eyebrows. "Or would that be a problem?"

She smiled and shook her head.

"I do take bigger risks with my cash, that's how you make the big payoffs."

"Well, I said it was my danger money."

"Ah."

She smiled.

"So, that's it for the excuses?"

"Thirty grand is a lot for an excuse just to talk to you." She raised an eyebrow and grinned, lifting the wine glass to her face as if she wasn't sure if she wanted to flirt or not. "I would expect something more for that, perhaps."

He smiled. "You're getting a trip to the theatre."

"Quite."

"So what have you been up to these twelve years?" asked Rake.

She was saved from answering by her food arriving. Rake wondered if he was going to watch her push another salad around her plate.

"Well, y'know, as I said, uni, grad scheme at Accenture, after that, swanning around Europe, making money."

"And not getting married."

She shrugged. "What about you?"

"I'm not married."

She smiled. "I know that."

"Well, I've been working."

She sighed and gestured with her wine glass. "So, tell me about work then."

"Would you rather know about my love life? Is that what you're getting at?"

She speared some slimy avocado. It slipped off the fork and she sighed. "That is hardly any of my business."

Rake grinned. "Well, y'know, I meet a lot of women, something about the Maserati attracts them."

"It's so strange to think of you as being rich, and, in some way, not strange at all." She grinned. "And you were never interested in safe bets when it came to women."

Rake raised his eyebrows. "Safe bets? You make it sound like an investment."

"It is, it's an investment of time."

"Not worth the paper it's printed on."

She said nothing and actually ate some of the avocado that was drowned in soy sauce.

"This, er... Rich guy, is he an investment to you?"

She raised an eyebrow at him. "We've been together a while now, if that's what you're asking."

"It fun?"

"Sometimes."

"He good in bed?"

She rolled her eyes.

"Oh, Helene, why do you always go for men that don't bother to fuck you?"

"What?"

"I can tell, I can tell when a woman isn't getting enough. She has that look around her eyes, and you were always quite a physical person."

"You don't know what the fuck you are talking about!"

"Where is he then?"

"Who?"

"Rich, it's a Friday night, and you're out with me."

"It's a Friday night and you're out with *me*."

"I cancelled a date."

"Fuck's sake, Rake, you sure know how to ruin one!"

He chuckled.

She speared some more avocado and chewed it angrily. "This food is shit."

"You're mad at me, I get that, but there's no need to take it out on the slimy green vegetable." Rake grinned at his wit.

"It's a fruit."

"Since when?"

She glanced at her plate. "Or it could be a nut, I s'pose.."

"You're the one with the biology degree."

She sighed and then leaned over to nick a forkful of his pasta. "I'm confiscating this"—she waggled it at him—"cos you're so fucking rude."

"We can swap if you want."

She frowned and then nodded, passing over the salad. "Enjoy."

Rake didn't think he needed to taste the salad to check that it was a manky as it looked. He smiled at her and topped up her glass.

"You trying to get me drunk?"

"I was trying to keep you sober actually."

"Why?"

"Why'd you think?"

She stared. "And you've given up already?"

"I've pissed you off, haven't I?"

"You always pissed me off," she muttered, twirling tagliatelle around the fork.

She ate the pasta quickly. Rake watched in silence, grinning slightly, until she finished.

"I knew you couldn't have a figure like that only eating crappy salads."

She slammed the fork onto the table. "Jeez, first you tell me I'm unfuckable, now you call me fat. You are such an arse!"

"I wasn't calling you fat, I like your figure."

"And now you're trying it on again. Do you have the slightest fucking clue what you want?"

"You?" He raised his eyebrows in a question.

"See, you're not even sure." She dabbed her mouth and then threw the napkin on the table. "Thanks for dinner, Rake. See you in another twelve years."

And with that she was up and walking out.

Rake took a moment to process what had just happened, then he was following her. He paused after a few steps and chucked a couple of fifties on the table. Then he was outside as she was hailing a cab.

"Helene, come on."

She ignored him and got into the cab. "Notting Hill," she said.

He got in straight after her. "No, the Old Vic."

"What the fuck? You think I want to go to the theatre

with you now?"

"Come on, Helene, I'm sorry I offended you."

"Where am I going, love?" the cabbie asked.

"The Old Vic," said Rake. Then he looked at Helene. "Look, we'll get a drink there and if you still want to fuck off, I'll hail you a cab."

"Very magnanimous of you. I already had a cab—"

The cabbie put his hand forward and incremented the meter by a few pounds.

"—and I'm more than capable of getting one all by myself, you know."

"And I'll buy you the drink. Can't say fairer than that."

She stared out of the window. The traffic lights changed from red to amber.

She sighed and shook her head. "All right, then, I'll admit I'm curious how much more you can fuck this evening up."

Rake grinned.

"The Old Vic then," said the cabbie, and they were off, flying through the traffic, cutting up pedestrians and training cyclists to have nerves of steel.

Exposure

1996: Helene's House, Plumstead

Helene had cleaned him up. She proved to be a dab hand with the disinfectant. Her mum had come in halfway through, asked a few pointed questions, got no answers, then had left and returned with a large glass of brandy for him.

The assessment wasn't good.

His jaw was bruised—not broken, he was pretty sure—but his lips were cut in two places. He had black eyes, but his nose wasn't broken. He had some pretty amazing bruises on his chest, cuts from the ladder which Helene had felt needed paper stitches. They probably needed more than that. But they'd hidden those from Helene's mum. Still, Helene's mum had floated the idea of going to casualty. But Rake didn't want to go.

He probably should have. His chest hurt with every breath. He probably had a few broken ribs, or maybe just bruised. But he didn't want the bastard to know he'd beaten him up bad enough that he was in hospital. Even if that cunt never found out, Rake would know.

Instead, he gritted his teeth, drank the brandy, and let

Helene clean him up. In the end, she got most the magnolia paint off with the disinfectant as well, but there were still bits stuck on him.

Then, before Helene's mum could realise that she was the adult in the situation and insist on taking him to hospital, he borrowed a t-shirt and walked home. It was now about eleven pm and even colder. He felt a bit better, from the brandy, and a bit worse, from seeing how badly he'd been beat up.

He got home and let himself in the back door. The light was on in the front room. Someone had left it on. He should have paid more attention, because the door opened and he saw his dad's face.

He should have stayed at Helene's.

"You! In here! Now!"

Fuck.

Rake moved as slowly as he thought he could get away with. He was pretty sure that whatever it was, his dad wouldn't beat him over it, not looking the way he did. And if his dad did—hell, if his dad kicked him across the floor again, then he'd end up in casualty with a fucking broken rib.

The last fucking thing he needed.

"What the fuck happened to you?" said his dad.

Rake shrugged, sending stinging pain across his chest.

"You been fighting?"

Was that not fucking obvious?

"Look at you," said his mother. "What sort of son have I raised? You lie to your parents, come home looking like shit, what the fuck were you doing?"

"Nuffink."

His dad shook his head. "Look, Seb, you are going down the job centre tomorrow and you are finding some work, OK? I won't have you lying around the house sponging off us no more."

They knew then.

His mother was waving a letter at him. "This is how I find out. You get yourself kicked out of school and don't have the guts to tell us. Why didn't you hand in any coursework?"

Rake shrugged.

"They said you've not been working. What have I done to deserve a lazy layabout son?"

"Dunno."

"Don't be smart with us," said his father.

He was just answering the question as honestly as he knew how.

"And that bloody school, they don't bloody tell us until they'd kicked you out." She shook her head. "And have you been hiding letters addressed to us?"

Rake shook his head.

"Now you're lying to your mother as well." She sounded petulant.

"I'm..." He decided it might be best to just examine the carpet.

"I have half a mind to go down there and bawl out that headmaster of yours. They should have let us know directly if you were having problems."

Rake raised his head. "I'll go back. I can do the Lower Sixth again. This time I won't fuck it up, I promise."

His parents glanced at each other.

"No," his dad said, and his mum nodded. "You're obviously not cut out for school, I thought that all along, but I thought, if he wants to try, let him try. But you didn't even fucking try, did you? And now you want to spend another two years dicking around, whilst we pay room and board?"

"You're seventeen now," said his mum. "It's time you take some responsibility for your life and start contributing to the household."

"You're going to the job centre tomorrow, got it?" said his dad. "And you're paying twenty quid a week rent from now on."

"Come on, that's all I get from the Co-op!"

"That's why you're going to get a proper job."

His mum nodded. "Wear a shirt, not one that's too nice, you'll get blood on it."

"Try an' get a 'pprenticeship or something. I could recommend you to the foreman, but only if you're gonna actually work. No one wants a lazy fucker. And it'll look bad on me if I recommend a layabout."

"Don't listen to them if they suggest the army," added his mother.

Rake sighed. "What if there's nothing else, will you forget about the rent then?"

She laughed. "There will be something else."

"The rent ain't negotiable," said his dad.

"What if I can't pay? What if I lose me job at the Co-op?" Rake reckoned he could swing that.

"Then you will be outside on the fucking streets by Christmas, you hear me? An' count yourself fucking lucky that you're in such a state that I don't feel like punishing you."

"I am hurt that you lied to us, Sebastian, hurt." His mum didn't look hurt, she looked like a prize fighter ready to take on the world. "Now get to bed, and think about what you've done."

Rake didn't hang about.

An Encounter

2008: The Old Vic, Lambeth

And they were in the bar of the Old Vic, all blond wood and globe lights. Rake was used to the place. He felt at home here. He never enviously looked at the black-and-white photos of actors that stared down at him. Well, hardly ever.

He bought Helene a glass of Tattinger. She raised her eyebrows, and he decided he needed a Laphroaig 25.

He smiled. "Shall we start again?"

She scowled momentarily, then relaxed. "This time I won't order the fucking salad."

He decided it best not to say anything about food.

"So you still come to places like this then?"

He nodded. "Market research. I'm an expert. I need to know who's who, who's hiring who, who's sleeping with who even. It's difficult, all these factors affect a company's share price, but it's all muddied together."

"What do you mean?" She seemed interested despite herself. And he smiled at her. That dress clung in all the right places.

"Well, a studio might have three good films coming

out—two shit ones, a mediocre one and a surprise indie hit. What you really want to do is bet on a movie, rather than a studio or their parent company. That's one of the things I've been working on."

"Really?"

He nodded. "A new financial instrument, but not one of those hideous maths things the quants on LSD make up. Mine's quite simple. You get people to buy stock in a film project, say, and they get a cut of the profits at the end. A lotta people are interested."

"Very clever."

"Simple, actually, all the best ideas are simple."

She smiled. "Is it better than acting?"

He was taken aback and realised that she was watching him closely. "I'm fucking acting every day of my life," he said, gulping at the whiskey. "So... y'know, it's all right."

There was a silence for a moment. She looked over the actors' portraits again, and Rake allowed himself a more thorough investigation of the clingy properties of wool.

She looked back and caught his eye. He grinned. She tilted her head to the side, and decided to continue with meaningless small talk. "You still see your mum?"

"Yeah." She weren't who he wanted to think about.

"She ever forgive you for leaving?"

"She didn't give a toss that I left. I go back from time to time so she can tell me how much more successful Cezek is than me."

Helene raised her eyebrows.

"So I always make sure I get her a really shit Christmas present and forget her birthday."

"What about your old man?"

Rake laughed. "I don't let him know how much money

I got. He asks for 'loans', you know? But if I gave him any he'd drink himself to death even quicker than he already is."

There was a pause.

"You really care about my family history, or is there something specific you're getting at?"

She shook her head. "You're a fucking abrasive person sometimes, Rake."

"Sorry, I won't be abrasive and tell you how good you look, I'll be polite and ask you how you fucking felt when your parents divorced, is that how you want it?"

"Jeez, Rake, that wasn't what I was trying to ask."

"Come on, everyone in Plumstead knows everyone else's business, so why bother to inquire about it?"

"Fuck's sake. I thought we could talk, that's all. We used to be able to talk about anything."

Rake examined his whiskey for a moment, then grinned. "You sure all you want to do is talk?"

She raised her eyebrows then. "You're acting."

He stared.

"Sorry. Forget I noticed."

"Forget you noticed? What the fuck?"

Helene downed what was left of her champagne. "I'm going now. Am I going to your flat or mine?"

At that point the first bell rang for the performance. "Mine."

They rode in the taxi back to the east end of the Docklands in silence. Rake hoped it was because they didn't want the taxi driver to hear what they had to say. When they got into the lift up to the penthouse Helene moved close to him and kissed him. She tasted sweet and of champagne. For a moment, Rake pondered how this was the first time he had kissed her, and yet it seemed strange to him that that fact was true.

Then they were on his floor and crossing the hallway. He grinned at her, taking another chance to check out her chest in the dress, then he was letting them into the flat. Another girl would pause and remark on something—the picture windows with a view of Canary Wharf in the distance, the tasteful black leather sofas, the fucking Britpop art on the walls—but Helene didn't even glance at it. She just put her arms around him, nibbled on his ear and whispered, 'Which way?'

"This way," he said, slamming his keys onto the coffee table. Penthouses didn't need to be locked. Who the fuck could get in?

They were walking towards the bedroom. Rake paused to put the lights on. He wanted to have a good view of this. He decided to take his time, he wanted to know what Helene's new body felt like under the wool, before he got to touch it without. She was more eager, trying to unbutton his shirt, but failing at the buttons for some reason.

He got impatient with wool and pulled her dress off. Underneath she was wearing black lacy lingerie that he had been able to pick up through the dress and some of those stocking things that stuck to a woman's legs by some miracle of science. He liked those things and started peeling one down her leg before getting distracted by the sight of her breasts in the bra. Rake took his time undressing her and Helene seemed content to let him. Then he decided that he really needed to taste her as well. Her skin was soft and smooth and scented with some fancy perfume, but he much preferred the smell of her that he could pick up underneath it, heady and earthy, musky and ready.

He decided to taste that part of her. Rake knew he was a good lover and wanted to make damn sure that Helene got the best impression of his skills. And there was nothing sexier than a woman enjoying herself. He made her come, her body buckling and fighting him, gasping and giving in. And then she decided to take control. He let her. He still had half his clothes on but she removed those in quick order, flinging them away. Then she was touching and teasing him—Jeeeeez, she'd learned some tricks—and then she moved on top of him, taking him slowly, driving down like it was tantric or some shit, squeezing him and keeping him on the very brink, taking him close, but not letting him go over until she was ready. And then she was, she was coming, he was responding and then there was nothing, he gripped on to her and felt everything he was, everything he had been, flowing out of him, into her. He heard himself saying something over and over, her name: "Helene, Helene, oh, Helene."

The mid-morning sun scraped across his eyelids. Rake sighed. He had forgotten to close the blinds.

He didn't open his eyes. He was mildly surprised to realise that he wasn't hungover, he wasn't on a comedown, he wasn't still high—he was just calm and feeling good. He ran his hands over Helene's shoulder. She was still asleep, he could tell by the gentle rise and fall of her stomach.

He had been right, she was a very physical person. And Jeez, if this Rich guy wasn't fucking her, he was a damned idiot.

In the night they'd lost all the covers. The sun was giving him a good view of Helene. He let his eyes roam over her, drinking her in, committing her to memory more strongly than a photograph ever could have done. Then he moved slightly and that was enough to wake her. Her breathing changed, but she didn't move. He kissed her gently on the forehead and she sort of purred, sort of moaned and stretched her arms lazily. "Fuck, I feel good," she said.

He smiled.

She opened her eyes and smiled back. "Morning."

"Hi."

And then he was kissing her again...

Afterwards she got up. He watched her walk across the room to her handbag, confident naked. She returned with a pack of Marlborough Lights and a lighter. She offered the pack to him. He took one, lazily observing her. The cheap plastic lighter finally sparked on the last attempt and she bent over it to light the cigarette then offered it to him. Trying to light the damned thing hurt his thumb. But he managed and took a deep drag on the cigarette.

"You still won't replace a lighter until it's beyond empty," he remarked, laughing.

She shrugged. "You still smoke rollies?"

"Fucking Camels or cigars."

She nodded and pulled her legs in to sit cross-legged.

"You all right?" he asked.

She tilted her head to the side, and then smiled. "Y'know, I think I am."

"Coffee?"

She nodded. "Mind if I take a shower?"

He pointed her to the bathroom. She didn't take long. When she came over to the breakfast bar she looked perfect. The smudged eye make-up was gone: Helene was now the sort of woman that carried make-up remover in her bag. She was dressed again in the tight dress, the stocking things, the three-inch heels. Her hair had been combed, polished, probably fucking hair-sprayed from tousled back into the smooth straight tin helmet look.

It was strange, to see her like that whilst he was only wearing his black silk robe. He grinned and turned back to the Kees van der Westen machine, fiddling with it to make a fantastic cappuccino. When he turned back to her, he saw she had her make-up bag out and was reapplying. He watched her for a moment, musing how intimate it was to watch her put her make-up on. Then he made his cappuccino and sat on the stool opposite her. She had the lipstick on now, and had drunk some of the cappuccino without leaving any on the cup, another miracle of science. She was just putting mascara on as he'd sat. Then she stopped, presumably finished. Her make-up applied with precision, she looked ready for the office.

She lit herself another cigarette. "Thanks for the coffee."

Rake nodded. "Sure." There was something strange in her demeanour: she was already leaving in her mind, walking out of the door, down the street, to wherever. She didn't look like the Helene he'd had in his bed only half an hour ago, she looked like the Helene that had walked into the restaurant, a stranger with the name of an old friend.

"What are your plans for today?" asked Rake. "You want, we could go out for brunch or something."

She smiled brassily. "I can't today. I gotta work. Lots to do."

"Of course."

She drained the last of her coffee and put her half-smoked cigarette in the ashtray. She stood up, picking up her bag and coat. "I'd better go."

And she was walking across his flat. He watched her for a moment, then jumped up and ran after her, opening the front door for her.

"Goodbye, Rake," she said, and she was off down the corridor. She didn't look back. The lift dinged and then she was gone. Rake shut the door and looked back at his flat. Her cigarette still smoked in the ashtray.

He was pretty certain he wouldn't see her again.

Liars

1996: Woodlands Estate, Plumstead

The job centre was shit. They had nothing he liked the look of and they didn't like the look of him. He asked about auditions and they shook their heads and talked about window cleaning and washing up in a restaurant or some shit. The advisor suggested to come back and sort out interviews when his face was healed up. She told him he'd be more successful if he could avoid getting into fights: as if that wasn't bloody obvious.

She offered to sign him up to the dole, but Rake didn't want to. Some sort of foolish pride wouldn't let him, and, he was pretty sure that his old man would beat him to a pulp if he found out.

So he filled in some forms for some real shit jobs and then did what most people did coming out of a job centre and fucked off to the pub.

For some perverse reason he called for Cezek on the way.

Cezek's mum's house was on the estate, and Rake got jeered at by some thirteen-year-old fuckers that hung around there, riding bikes up and down, smoking and setting fire to garbage. The door opened and Cezek's mum stared at the bruises.

"Don't fucking get 'im into any trouble, Rake."

"We're just going to the pub."

She turned her back and hollered, "Cezek, get down 'ere," then sodded back off to her TV.

Cezek bounded down the stairs and stopped at the door. He laughed uproariously. "What the fuck happened to you?"

"Let's just go to the pub, OK?"

"Yeah, let me get changed first." Cezek was in his work clothes—shiny shoes, pressed black trousers, stripy shirt and a wide purple tie. He looked like a fucking estate agent and not a trustworthy one. It always amazed Rake that anyone would buy anything from him.

Rake waited just inside the door, checking out how bad he looked in the mirror.

Cezek half jumped, half fell down the stairs again. Now he was dressed in black jeans and a Marilyn Manson t-shirt. *One day*, Rake thought, *the fucker'll miss the stairs and just jump the whole fucking stairwell and smash into the front door.*

As they walked to the pub, Rake told Cezek everything. Then, after checking that his dad wasn't in there, they bought themselves a pint and sat as far away from his dad's mates as possible. This put them crammed in by the pool table and the front door that no one used.

"So what are you going to do?" asked Cezek.

"I'm gonna fucking kill 'im!" Rake looked around. No one was paying any attention. "For all I know he could 'ave killed Jane already, but either way, he's gonna end up leaving her alone."

Cezek nodded and then grinned. "So you've come to

me."

Rake looked at the foam islands on top of his beer. "I... I dunno..."

But he knew he couldn't take Terry out alone. Not easily. Rake was pretty sure that he had more brains than Terry, but not having a gun, he would have to get in close for any ambush.

And if it all went wrong, Terry would beat him into a fresh plot up at Highfield Cemetery.

"It's all right, blood." Cezek punched him on the arm. "Not a problem. We'll take this fucker out easy, then you and Lise can live happily ever after above the curry house."

Rake shook his head. "That's not why, I mean, he don't deserve her—"

Cezek was wearing a slight smile.

"—and he'll fucking kill her if I don't do something. The guy's a fucking psycho, he treats her like a sack of shit."

Cezek nodded wisely. "Sometimes you gotta take what you want."

"That's not it at all! She doesn't want him around."

"Then why's she there then? You ever ask that? They don't live together, why don't she tell him to fuck off when he comes round?"

"I... I dunno, all right? But that's not the point."

"Course not, we gotta get the fucker that did that to you." Cezek gestured at Rake's face. "We'll do it tomorrow night."

At the point, Seth wandered into the bar and saw that they'd started the Friday drinking session early.

"You all right, Rake?"

Rake nodded.

"Get him a whiskey or summink, would you?" said Cezek.

Seth frowned at him then went up to the bar. Cezek pulled on Rake's shirt, which hurt the ribs he'd now decided were bruised. "Keep this between us. I don't trust that fucker. The way he looks at me sometimes, I wouldn't put it past him to dob us in."

Rake pulled Cezek's hands off his clothes and moved back. "What, Seth? Go to the filth? You gotta be fucking kidding me. No way."

Cezek eyed Seth's back belligerently. "Naaah, I dunno, that's one untrustworthy fucker right there."

Shortly after, everyone else turned up. Helene manoeuvred herself next to Cezek, then leaned across him to ask Rake how his injuries were. Cezek took the opportunity to drop an ice-cube from Rake's whiskey down Helene's neck, which led to her jumping around and ripping her coat off to try and get the damned thing out before she was completely soaked.

"What the fuck happened to you?" asked Gary, once he and Stacie had arrived. Helene completely blanked Stacie and only said hello to Gary, but Stacie didn't seem to notice.

"Nothing, all right?" said Rake.

Helene smiled at him sympathetically.

"And why the shirt?" asked Stacie.

"I been down the job centre."

"At last," said Gary in a self-satisfied way, and Rake wanted to punch the stupid fucker's face in.

"What made you do that?" asked Stacie.

Rake sighed. "Me parents said they'd kick me out if I didn't pay some fucking rent." Rake emptied out his pocket. Two quid fifty, a bus ticket, a very thin-looking bag of baccy, some filters and some papers. "An' that's all I got left in the world."

"Your dad did that to you?" asked Seth.

Rake shook his head.

"Yes," Cezek said. He gave Rake a significant look.

Rake shrugged and looked down. No way they could tie them to Terry if they didn't know about Terry at all.

But his dad had never beat him that bad.

When he looked up Helene was looking from Rake to Cezek in confusion.

"Shit, man," said Seth, shaking his head.

"It's not as bad as it looks..." Rake muttered. It was worse.

Then, by some miracle, everyone got the idea that he didn't want to talk about it. Although, the first time for a while, Gary and Stacie put themselves out to buy him a drink.

Helene kept looking at him in confusion, but then Cezek distracted her. The stupid fuck started an argument about some shit, a pound owed, that ended with him telling her she was ugly. She sat there with a sour-grapes face for a while until Cezek started chatting her up again. Then Cezek had to leave, and wanted to walk home with Helene. Then he made a fuss about how long she was taking to pack up and he walked off on his own. She ran after him and returned to the pub about twenty minutes later.

"He's gone." Her eye make-up was all smudged.

"That's not a bad thing," remarked Seth. "Maybe he's gone forever."

She shook her head. "No, it is, it is. He's not home, his mum says she ain't seen him."

"He's just gone off in a sulk somewhere, just to make

you feel bad about it," said Rake.

She shook her head. "Shall we go look for him?"

"Don't bother," Gary said. "We're going now, we'll call you if we find him dead in a ditch."

"Dead in a ditch?"

"Don't wind her up," said Stacie. "Just fucking move, would you? I gotta be up early for work tomorrow."

And they were off. Seth and Rake looked at each other.

"What should I do?" asked Helene. "You think he's in trouble?" *The guy is trouble.*

"He's just sulking up on the common," said Seth.

"You reckon?" And she was off.

"Shit. Why does she always run around after that stupid cunt?"

Rake shrugged.

"He treats her like utter shit and she just laps it up like it's hot chocolate."

Rake sighed. "You think I should go and find her?"

Seth shrugged. "Dunno, but I'm fucking off now."

At that point the barman rang time. Rake sighed and trudged towards the common. He wandered along the dip, expecting to find her there, but she wasn't. Then he just ambled aimlessly. He would have gone home, but he didn't want to get there until his parents were so deeply asleep that they wouldn't get woken up. His dad had bionic ears and was moody when his sleep was disturbed.

Then he saw them—Cezek and Helene, sitting side by side on the bench press, silhouetted against the orangey night sky. He was downhill from them. He paused, standing under a tree in the shadows, curious.

"Come on, Cezek, I didn't mean it," Helene was saying. She sounded like she'd been crying, snuffly and snotty.

"Yes, you did, you know you did."

Rake wondered what Helene was being accused of doing.

"But... I didn't mean... y'see..."

Then Cezek took her hand and she stared at him. Rake hadn't ever seen the fucker display any tenderness before.

"You are so stupid, Helene, y'know?" She actually nodded. "But y'know, it's OK. I put up with stuff from you, you know?"

"Yeah." She sounded defeated.

"I'm like that, magnanimous. I take a lot of shit from you." Rake thought it was the other way around. "And you know why?"

She lifted her head to look at Cezek, then shook it.

He didn't say anything, but then suddenly moved forward to kiss her. Rake stared at his feet. When he looked up she was just staring at Cezek.

Cezek laughed, letting go of her hand. "Shit, you are such a fucking idiot."

"Why? Why do you say that?"

"I try and kiss you and you move."

"You... I didn't know."

She moved forward to kiss him back. Cezek pushed her away. "No, forget it."

"But... what? Why?"

Cezek got up. "Helene..." He looked down.

"What's the matter?" She got up and wrapped her arms around him. He pushed her away, and she stumbled and landed heavily on the floor.

"Just fucking forget it, OK?"

"But Cezek—"

"I said forget it!"

"But it's OK."

"No, it fucking isn't, OK? Just leave me alone, you whore!"

"I'm... I'm not a whore! Don't you dare say that! You've got no excuse! You, you, you just push and push—"

"Don't speak to me like that. Don't you dare!"

"But you—the way you speak to me!"

"Don't think you can tell me what to do, Helene."

Rake could see her jaw moving as she tried to eat her lip.

"Look, I'm sorry, Cezek, I'm sorry." And she was up and walking towards him. "I'm sorry."

She put her arms out to hug him. He stepped back and slapped her in the face. She stood there, holding her cheek, her mouth open, the tears picked up by the street-lights.

"Just forget it." And with that Cezek was striding off.

Rake didn't move. Helene crumpled up into a ball, sort of curled her legs up and crouched. And she sobbed.

Shit. He counted to ten, and then counted to ten again. *Fuck.* And he was on the path. She noticed him, backlit against the streetlights. She didn't look like she recognised him but made no attempt to move.

"Who's there?" She didn't sound like she cared.

"Rake."

She lifted her head. "What you doing here?"

He shrugged. "Just out walking, y'know?"

"You seen Cezek?"

"No, was he here?"

She stared at him then, and he wasn't sure if she believed him. Then she shook her head. "Why the fuck did you lie about who beat you up?"

"No reason."

"Come off it, Rake, why'd you lie?"

"I... I just did, OK?"

She sighed. "All fucking liars," she muttered.

"What?"

"You're all fucking liars, don't think I don't know!"

His breath went like he was sucker-punched.

"Just talking shit to me and..." Then she was sobbing again.

"What?" Rake was over to her and sitting on the bench. "What have we been lying about?"

"You and Cezek. You're both lying about who beat you up and I don't know why, but I ask him and he goes off on one, y'know? He keeps telling me he doesn't lie and I should know that, but I know he lied, I know it!"

Rake stared at her. He didn't know what to do so he rolled her a rollie and handed it to her. She looked at it.

"It's one of his triggers, I know that. You don't call him short, never speak badly of his mum and you don't accuse him of lying and he's fine."

Rake didn't know that Cezek had taken the effort to qualify and announce his excuses for anger.

"But when I know he's lying..."

There was a silence. Rake looked at her, hunched over, squatting on the floor and looking at the cigarette. Lacking any clue of what to do, he rolled one for himself.

"He kissed me, you know."

"Really?" Rake couldn't admit why he doubted that.

"Sort of." She sighed. "He tried to. But I moved and he kissed me on the nose." She shook her head. "And then he gave up. What sort of person gives up at that point?"

"You... er, ever kiss him before?" Rake passed her his Zippo lighter. It had a Harley Davidson logo on it.

"That was the first time, and I fucked it up." Then she was sobbing again.

Rake shook his head. She stopped sobbing and blew her nose on a tissue and then lit up the rollie.

"You didn't fuck it up," he said. "There's something wrong with Cezek. You should find yourself a better guy."

She laughed. She sounded a lot older than seventeen when she laughed like that. "Why would a better guy take me?"

"What the fuck do you think is wrong with you?"

She sighed. "Everything. I'm stupid and ugly."

"Jeez, Helene, you're not stupid, you're the smartest of all of us. You're the only one going to university, for starters." She looked at him. "And you're not ugly," he muttered to his shoes.

When he looked up she was looking out at the city lights. Her cigarette had gone out. He handed her the Zippo. She looked surprised that he was there, but took it and lit up.

"Why do women put up with this shit?" he asked. She looked at him in confusion. "Come on, Cezek slapped you, and you're fine with that."

"You saw that?" Her eyes were luminous in the dark. "Maybe."

"Fuck! What the fuck? Where were you?"

"Look, I just wandered up as he walked off."

"Jesus."

"Helene, he slapped you, why don't you just tell him to fuck off?"

She sighed then took a deep drag on his cigarette. "You don't understand."

"I do understand. You could do better."

She laughed. "I don't deserve better," she muttered.

"And anyway, he was mad, that's all, cos I accused him of lying. I know that's something that pisses him off. I didn't even mean to accuse him, I just asked why... But he's told me before not to question what he says." Rake was watching her now. "And, you know..." She sort of smiled. "He kissed me tonight." She shrugged. "Or tried to."

"Helene, seriously, don't bother with him."

"But I think I love him."

Rake felt disgusted and couldn't look at her. He regarded the city lights. And she was crying again, softly, into her hands.

Rake shook his head. "Come on, let's get you home, OK?"

"He might come back."

"I doubt it. Look, Helene, Cezek's not the kind of guy who puts himself out for others."

She scowled at him then. "You think I don't know what sort of person he is? I know him better than anyone."

Rake stared at her.

"So I don't get where you're coming from with all this portentous shit. He's told me things he's not told anyone. He told me so."

Rake stared at her. *No...*

"Helene..."

She didn't know. She couldn't.

She curled herself up tighter into a ball, hugging her knees to her face. "Why is he like this to me? He acts like he loves me, and then he just fucks it all up."

Rake just looked at her miserably.

"I don't understand."

He stood up. "Come on, Helene, it's fucking freezing out here, let's go back."

She didn't move for what seemed like ages, and then she sighed and unfolded herself. They had turned and walked a few steps before they saw him.

"What the fuck you doing here, Rake?" asked Cezek. His hands were fisted and the streetlights were behind him so Rake couldn't see his face. Rake shrugged.

"Cezek!" Helene sounded grateful.

She jogged over to him and Cezek whispered something to her that caused her shoulders to sag. She shook her head and then looked back at Rake. Then she whispered something to Cezek.

"I'll see you tomorrow, Rake," said Cezek, then he turned and Helene followed him without even looking back at Rake. Rake watched them for a while. They walked close, but didn't touch, didn't hold hands, didn't hug...

But he felt that they were going out now.

History

2008: A Bar in Soho

Months had passed. Rake had been persuaded, or maybe tricked, into conducting a meeting with Cezek in a bar. The fucker was still bugging him and taking up far more of his time than he deserved. But it was a lot of money and Cezek let him do what he liked with it. Sure, Cezek thought he was making the decisions, but Rake had discovered that Cezek was relatively easy to persuade. It was a matter of making out that something was a bad idea, a bit risky, a bit dangerous and that Rake wouldn't do it for anyone else, and Cezek went for it. Rake wasn't really sure what he was trying to accomplish—was he trying to lose Cezek his money, or was he trying to make a big fee out of him?

So he was sitting at a table, somewhat morosely watching the girls up at the bar. They were gorgeous and checking him out, or he thought they might be. Hell, they looked dressed up and ready to be plucked from the bar...

Shit. He looked down and ran his finger over the table top, leaving smeary marks.

Cezek sat down. He was grinning. "A good bar this. Nice hos hanging around." *Fucker.* "What's up? You're not worried about this American thing?" Rake shook his head. "You think I should be?" Cezek was scowling.

"Why? That's the American property market, it's not the same here."

"All them cheap loans, Fanny fucking Mae and that shit, all to fucking idiots."

"It's not as easy to get a mortgage here, I'm sure you'll be fine," sighed Rake. He wasn't thinking about houses.

Cezek nodded. "Y'know, I've been thinking, it was kinda interesting to meet you again. I'm gonna seek out the rest of the gang."

Rake eyed him sharply. "You already know the rest of the gang, you told me about them."

Cezek shook his head. "Not that gang. I'm going to seek out Helene. She's in London somewhere. I googled her. Working for Accenture. I thought I found her on Facebook, but she didn't reply to my mail. It looked like her, except with blondeish hair..."

Rake was staring at him in horror. "Not Helene."

"'Scuse me?" Cezek looked like he was mortally offended that someone would speak to him like that. He raised his eyebrows, causing his forehead to scrunch up.

"Not Helene. Leave her alone."

"What the fuck? Who the fuck do you think you are?"

"Just..." What could he say? The truth? There was no way Helene would be interested in Cezek. She wasn't that sort of woman any more. She didn't need protecting any longer.

She didn't need Rake.

"I don't know..." Rake looked over at the bar again. This time he didn't even register the women there.

Cezek stared him out. Then relaxed. "You know nothing. Me and Helene, we were tight." Rake knew. "We were fucking tight." Cezek smiled. "I shouldn'ta left her..." He looked troubled. "I did a lot for that bitch. A lot." He sniffed. "An' she didn't appreciate it, just fucking blanked me..." He gulped his beer. "She owes me."

"She doesn't owe you anything."

Cezek's eyes flashed dangerously. "I'd stop that right now if I were you, Rake. I let you get away with a lot of shit, just cos we're old mates, but don't fucking push it."

Rake started calculating the odds he'd get punched. He was putting it fifty-fifty, a punch or a laugh. He was in a bad mood. "She won't want to hear from you. She's had more than enough of your shit to last a lifetime. She'll just tell you to fuck right off." *This is one account he would say good riddance to.*

Cezek laughed and pounded him on the back. "You're a fucker, Rake, a real fucker. I tell you to leave it, and you just fucking won't, will you?" Suddenly, there was no laughter in Cezek's eyes. "Stupid fucker." Rake stared him out. "Still, we're mates, we gotta history, y'know? And that counts for a lot."

Decaying Tarmac

1996: Alleyway Behind Welling Station

They were that eager to build more skyscrapers in the Docklands that someone was paying for builders round the clock and Terry worked the night shift. Rake was pretty sure from what Jane had mentioned that he finished around five am and then headed home on the train.

If the fucker was working that Friday night, he'd be getting off the train in Welling at six am on Saturday. During the week the place would be full of commuters, all bright-eyed and bushy-tailed squirrels, but six am Saturday was another thing entirely. The place was empty, deserted: the suburbs were sleeping off Friday night's excesses.

So Rake and Cezek were milling around. There were two exits from the station—the main one you'd use to walk to Welling High Street, and the exit to the car park. From the car park a set of steps led you directly into the suburbs. From there, you could turn right and walk along an almost abandoned road, the back of a church, a shut-down nursery, a bloody family planning clinic. The road was mostly made of chunks of rock and stone, rotted city stuff. Rake wondered if this was what happened when tarmac degraded. There were abandoned tyres and bits of two-by-four around probably nicked from the lumber yard up the road, and cycle tracks. During the day, kids played here, enjoying the chance to fuck around with the sort of things their parents wouldn't want them to play with. Tetanus, for example.

It was a shit road. It felt like the end of civilization.

And it was the quickest route from the station to Jane's flat.

Cezek was sitting on a couple of the tyres and smoking, quiet for once. There were no streetlights down there, of course, just the blue-white glow that escaped from the distant platform.

There was a whoosh and a screech and Cezek was bathed in the staccato light of a train going past. Then it was gone, off to Bexleyheath, the clack, clack, clack of the damn thing gaining speed lost into the night.

"It might be this one," said Rake.

Cezek just nodded and then scrubbed his cigarette out.

Rake looked around nervously and picked up a bit of old two-by-four. The wood was rough and he got splinters. Still, better splinters than getting his ribs smashed in.

"Yeah, this'll do, this'll do," he said, more to say something than anything else.

Cezek shrugged. Then they both looked up the alley, hearing footsteps. By the city glow they could make out the silhouette of a man mountain heading their way. His shoulders were slumped and his steps slow, but Rake recognised the silhouette.

"It's him," Rake said. Cezek's eyes were gleaming in

the soft light. He was watching Terry's lumbering steps intently. "Did you hear me? That's him."

Cezek swivelled his eyes over and nodded as if Rake were a complete idiot. And Rake wondered if Cezek cared who the fucker coming up the path was.

Cezek took a few steps back against the fence. Now he was mostly hidden by the shadow of the trees. Rake copied him and stepped back against the barbed wire fence that marked the back of the church.

It was still night, but Terry might have seen them by the city glow. He didn't even lift his head. He was moving on the automatic pilot born of a twelve-hour shift. And then he was on them and Rake swung the two-by-four across his back.

Terry stumbled, but didn't fall. He was up, quick and turning.

"You fucker!" He recognised Rake and swung a round-house at his chin. Rake didn't defend, intent on bring-ing the wood down on Terry's head, his blow weakened as Terry's blow had gotten in first and pushed him back.

Rake made to whack Terry with the wood again, but Terry hit Rake's arm, knocking the wood aside. Cezek punched Terry in the side of the head, and then Rake fol-lowed up with a straight chin jab.

Terry was not a soft man, though. He turned, punched Cezek in the gut and pushed him away. Then he wheeled back to Rake—either he'd decided that Rake was the threat because he was taller, or he just wanted another chance at him. Rake stood his ground and punched Terry in the head. Terry shot a quick punch to Rake's chin, snapping his head back, then pummelled his fist into Rake's side, getting Rake's bruised ribs perhaps more by luck than by judgement.

Rake sank to his knees, a huddled-up ball of pain. Then Terry was kicking him—kicking him in the stomach, kicking him in the head. Rake curled up around his ribs, one hand over his head, taking the brunt of most the blows.

Then there was a thunk and it stopped.

Rake took in a sharp, shuddering breath.

More wet thunks.

Rake sort of stood, bent over, one arm wrapped around his middle, like someone with severe food poisoning. With difficulty, he lifted his head.

Cezek was hammering Terry with the wood. His first blow had got the fucker round the back of his head and now Terry was on the floor, his hands held up to defend him.

There was blood on the wood.

Cezek brought the wood down again. Terry's nose looked like chopped steak. Terry tipped his head forward and Cezek kicked him in the chest. Terry sprawled onto his back, landing on discarded timber.

Cezek turned and grinned at Rake, then walked over to Terry slowly. The guy was out cold, his breath coming in little bloody bubbles from what was left of his nose. Cezek raised the wood up above Terry's head.

"Cezek!" gasped Rake, trying to stand up straight.

Cezek looked back at him curiously.

"Stop!"

Cezek laughed. "Stop? Are you crazy? I thought you wanted to kill this fucker?"

Rake looked at Terry. *The guy is a fucker, he certainly doesn't deserve Jane, but does he deserve to die?*

"Just leave it, OK? He's got the message, he won't be seeing her no more."

"Leave it? You crazy?"

Rake nodded. "Cool it."

"You sure? What if he goes to the cops?"

Rake laughed. "He won't fucking go to the cops, they can lock him up for what he did to Jane."

Cezek looked thoughtful. He hefted the two-by-four above Terry's face, as if he was testing the properties of the air there. "He know who you are?" Rake shook his head. "She know where you live?" Rake shook his head. Cezek nodded. "I think you're a fucking idiot, but it's your call. This was your favour, you know?" Cezek was eyeing him. "Consider us even."

Rake just stared at him.

Cezek grinned. "Now let's fucking scarper, shall we?" He dropped the two-by-four right next to Terry's head. The fucker didn't move. His breath sounded chunky, like he was breathing through bits of cartilage.

It was a two-mile walk back to Plumstead. They hurried down the street, past Jane's flat. Rake even looked up at it as he passed it, but he didn't want to turn up there like this. He was bent double and bloody, and Jane didn't need any more violence in her life.

So they carried on. When they got to the field the sun started to rise. The air was cigarette-ash grey and it hung around the blackened grass like smoke. Rake stopped at the first bench he came to.

"What the fuck you doing?"

"I... I think I'm hurt."

Cezek looked all around him, as if there were people watching. In the distance, Rake could see a lone dog walker.

"Fuck's sake, Rake, you can't pull this shit now. You can't go to hospital, they'll realise."

"I'm fine, OK? I'm fucking fine..." Rake's teeth were gritted and his breaths short.

Cezek nodded. "Come on." He pulled him up.

Rake groaned from the pain and then he was walking, not exactly supported by Cezek, more dragged.

"Shit, I gotta stop," moaned Rake. He was walking like a fucking gastric flu patient.

"You ain't stopping," said Cezek.

They left the green space and were in the Plumstead suburbs—home, for want of a better word. They passed an abandoned burnt-out car, still acrid in the cold morning air.

"No, I'm really bad, I think I gotta stop..."

Cezek leaned Rake up against the car. "What you gonna do?"

"I gotta go to hospital."

Cezek blew air out of his teeth. "Look, mate, the favour was beating up that cunt, y'know? I can't be involved in this shit if you're gonna bring the pigs in. I'll lose me fucking job."

"Fucker."

"Yeah, well, you shouldn't'a let him beat you so bad."

And with that Cezek turned his back on him and walked off with a false nonchalance.

"Fucker!" Rake shouted after him, or tried to, but it wasn't much of a shout. Cezek just waved his hand at him and then turned the corner. "Fuck!" Rake summarised to himself.

And then he was moving, staggering like a drunk. He had a plan. His house and Helene's house were approximately the same distance from where he was, in different directions.

He turned towards Helene's. Helene's was a flat route,

his own house was up two fucking hills. It was a slow, painful stagger. No one seemed to be up and around, the suburbs were quiet, he even startled a balding fox from its investigations of someone's bin bags.

This was bad. He was gonna end up dead in someone's geraniums and get found by the fucking paperboy.

He carried on walking. He was near the common now, he could see it up ahead. Helene's house was only round the corner.

He slipped on some leaf mulch or a used condom or last night's fucking kebab or something, and crashed onto the ground, his arm under him so he couldn't break the fall. His jaw did that. His head rang with black flashing lights and then it was dark.

––––––––––––––

The first thing Rake noticed was the smell—not wet grass, but disinfectant. He was lying on his back. He opened his eyes. Everything was white. Maybe he was dead. He screwed his eyes up and opened them again. White ceiling, pale green walls. Shit, he was in hospital.

Rake raised his head and looked towards his feet and then wished he hadn't. There was a copper—tall, dark and official-looking—his dad and his mum. Her makeup was all smudged and she looked mad.

"Uh... Hi, Mum," Rake said.

His mum shook her head, crying. "I'm upset with you, Sebastian, I'm glad you're alive, but I am fucking disappointed in you."

Fuck.

Rake cautiously moved his arms. He wasn't handcuffed to the bed. Did that mean the filth didn't know what he'd done or was he that badly injured that they didn't think he could run? Rake's body was a drum 'n' bass throbbing of pain. He reckoned he could walk, but not out-limp a copper.

"Sebastian," said the copper, "can you tell me what happened?"

Rake shook his head. "Uh... Didn't see nuffink, officer."

"Who beat you up?"

"Not sure, officer."

"Listen, son. Do you want to press charges?"

Rake shook his head vehemently.

The copper flipped his notebook shut with a snap.

"That's it? That's all you're gonna do?" protested his mum.

The copper nodded. "We've got no witnesses. If he changes his mind about pressing charges then bring him down Plumstead nick." He handed Rake's mother a card. "And ask for me."

She nodded and the copper walked out. Rake relaxed.

Then his dad was sitting next to him, perched in one of those high-seated chairs with high arms and alien-flower patterns that old ladies liked. "You win, son?"

Rake grinned. "You think this is bad, you should'a seen the other guy!"

Rake's dad smiled.

"What the hell are you telling him now?" said his mother. "This isn't funny. He was nearly killed."

"A coupl'a broken ribs isn't nearly killed. I had worse in my day."

"Bloody hell! That's what you think this is? For fuck's sake, don't go encouraging him, I've had quite enough of being called to hospital bedsides in the early morning." His mother waggled her index finger at Rake. "You need to straighten yourself out, Sebastian, cos the way you're going you'll end up nothing but a nobody just like your father!" And with that she swept the green plastic privacy curtains aside and clacked her heels across the ward.

Rake's dad looked like he'd been sucker-punched and Rake wondered if that might have been kinder.

His dad sat there for a while, saying nothing, slowly rolling himself a cigarette. He left that on the bedside table and rolled another.

"You'll be let out this afternoon," he said finally. "It ain't all that bad."

Rake nodded. Then he saw Helene through the gap in the curtains. She sped up.

"Rake! You all right?"

Rake smiled at her. "Sure."

His dad got up. "Just gonna have me a fag break, I'll be back in twenty." Then he pulled the curtains shut as tight as they would go, which didn't actually conceal anything.

Helene perched on the edge of the seat his father had vacated. "What the fuck happened? Where's Cezek?"

Rake sighed. "Did you find me?"

She shook her head. "Bob down the road tripped over you on his way to work, and then there was ambulances and coppers and Marie went out to see what was going on, an' then she came back to get me! I thought it was like..." She shook her head. "An' you were all unconscious. I thought you was dead, frozen stiff or summink!"

"I don't think I was that cold."

"They reckoned you coulda had hypothermia."

"I'm fine, just me ribs." They hurt. Rake wasn't going to be playing tennis for a while.

"What about Cezek? I know he was out with you last night, and I went to his house. His mum hadn't seen him—

"

Fucker's lying low.

"—is he as bad as you? Out there, somewhere..." She was chewing at her lip and staring through the pane.

"What, you think I would leave him if he was?"

She stared at him then, tears forming at the corners of her eyes.

"Fucking Cezek's fine."

She smiled, looking relieved.

"He was with you, then?"

Rake nodded.

"So what happened? Was it Lise's boyfriend?"

Rake nodded. "Big, ugly fucker..."

"How'd he find you?"

"Helene, there been anyone else brought in? Have the cops been asking about... anything?"

"Like what?"

Like a fucking bear of a man beaten to shit in a crappy alleyway.

"I don't know."

She shook her head. "You tell the coppers about Terry?"

"Course not."

"But if he's beating up on Lise—"

"Pigs ain't no use to anyone. Anyway, she'll be OK now. Terry ain't gonna bother her no more."

Consequences

1996: Above a Curry House, Welling

Rake was out of hospital that afternoon. His mum grounded him for his own rest. On the third day he pissed her off enough that she let him go out and he was off across the field, back to Jane's house.

She didn't sound that happy to see him.

He walked into her flat and put his arms around her. "Are you OK? I'm sorry I couldn't get back here earlier, I came as soon as I could."

"Seb, I gotta go, visiting hours are only 'til four."

"What?"

"Some fucking thugs put Terry in the hospital, he's up at Sidcup—" A different one from where Rake had lain. "—an' I gotta go see him."

"Are you insane? He beat you up! Now you're free, you see? How long's he gonna be in there for? You could move, even, then he'll never find you."

"He needs me! I can't walk away now, leaving him in that state!"

"Yes, you can. Think about what he did to you! This is your chance to get away from him forever."

She sighed. "I don't know what you're trying to protect me from—"

"Him!" *Is that not obvious?*

"I don't need to be protected from him."

"He beat you up, smashed your things, punched you in the face. Come on, Jane, surely you can see he's a shit."

Jane slapped him. "Don't speak that way about Terry! I love him, he's a good man, OK? It's just the drink sometimes, that's all."

Rake just stared at her, his mouth open.

"And now he needs me. He needs me more than anyone."

"Fuck's sake, what's wrong with you?"

She sighed. "Look, Seb, just turn around and walk out that door. Don't come back."

"What? What about us?"

She laughed then. It was a laugh that sounded like it had matured for eighty years. "There is no us, Seb. I told you it was just sex, didn't I? You can't say I didn't tell you."

"But you wanted me to move in."

"I was emotional, upset, I thought Terry had left me."

Rake frowned then, finally getting it.

She took a few steps back, her hands fluttering up to her face to worry at her hair like birds in a hedge.

"I did all this for you, you know. Everything. To save you from this." He gestured at the flat, thinking about how it had looked when Terry had smashed all the ornaments. "And you don't want to leave? I don't get it, I really don't. I don't understand women who just put up with this shit, running around, lapping it up like hot chocolate..."

Rake paused then.

"What did you do for me, Seb?" Jane's eyes were narrowed.

Rake scoped out the carpet.

"It was you! You were one of the fucking thugs that beat Terry up! What'd'ja do, invite your mates along? He said there was like ten of the buggers."

"You know where I've been, Jane? You know why I didn't come to see you sooner? I was in the hospital. Your boyfriend broke my fucking ribs!"

"Well, I hope it bloody hurt!"

"But I did it for you!"

"Get out, get out now, before I call the fucking pigs!" And then she was hitting him, sort of batting him in the head. It didn't hurt but Rake retreated to the open door.

"But..." He stopped. There was nothing to say. Jane's face was like a shop with the shutters down. He turned and walked away down the stairs.

"An' don't you ever come back here again!" she yelled at him out of the door. Then the door slammed.

"Fuck," he muttered, holding onto his ribs as he stepped out into the cold.

Questions

2008: Rake's Penthouse, Poplar

It was ten pm and Rake was sitting in his flat. Not lounging in the La-Z-Boy with a beer, not perched up at the breakfast bar with an espresso, not leaning on the bar with a martini, not even sat at the ergonomic rocking stool in front of the Appleglass table—he was sitting on the floor, his back against the window, his long legs in front of him, staring at a laptop.

It didn't look good.

Nothing looked good.

He'd never seen anything quite like this. Everything was going down. Nothing seemed safe. Fuck, he even thought about investing in fucking gold, it was that bad. Everyone was scared. No one had a clue how much bad debt they had, or how much bad debt anyone else had, so no one was trusting anything. Every bank was hoarding—they'd all turned into fucking Scrooge-like pensioners and the money that used to slosh around the City was still, stagnant and stinking.

Rake sighed.

People were scared, even the fucking public were

scared. What did people do when scared? Now was the time to invest in movies—good, wholesome romances, fluffy action movies, that was what people wanted in times like this. Larger-than-life heroes overcoming terrible odds and winning the girl. They would switch WholeFoods for Tescos, Carluccio's for Pizza Hut and foreign holidays and meals out for red lipstick and champagne.

Rake started making a list of which studios had the best crop of action movies and romances in production. Then he leaned back and sighed, unconcerned about the visible drop behind him. Too long spent at the top of skyscrapers. The city below held no fear for him—there was glass to stop him falling, and the damned drop seemed like nothing more scary than a projected image.

Rake jolted at the sound of his phone, an ill-advised samba totally not fitting his mood. He picked it up, not even bothering to glance at the number.

"Hello?" His irritation crackled on the radio waves.

"Rake, I'm in a taxi heading to yours. If you want to tell me to turn around, now's your chance."

It was Helene, speaking like she was throwing the fucking gauntlet down.

"Uh..." Rake wished he could be cooler than this.

"Well?"

Rake slammed his laptop shut. "I'm all yours, Helene."

She hung up and he was left staring at the phone. *Where was she? In a taxi, obviously, why would she lie, but where? Just outside her flat? Hyde Park Corner? Outside his flat?*

He stood, moving up onto the balls of his feet and back down again. He paced up and down, pausing by the window each time to peer down, despite the fact it was useless—he could see the entire fucking city of London, the south in front of him, the Docklands to the west, but he couldn't see his own front door.

After about two minutes he could stand it no longer and pulled his shoes on and headed down, hoping that she wasn't in the lift going the other way. As he descended, he held onto his phone as if it were an oxygen gauge, checking it every second to see if he still had enough to get him back up to the surface.

Then he was in the plush lobby, all pink and white Florence marble, polished to a shine, with little lights to make it sparkly, Italian leather-edged mirrors on the walls, chrome ashtrays and the doorman who nodded at him and opened the door. He shook his head and paced a bit. Then he asked if the doorman had seen a petite blonde, just in case she had gone past him and forgotten his number. The doorman shook his head and Rake was pulling out a Camel and lighting it, pacing up and down his own fucking lobby.

Ten minutes later, a taxi arrived. Rake tossed his second half-smoked cigarette into the ashtray and stopped pacing. He couldn't see who it was, and then Helene stepped out, her hair shining, red heels, camel trenchcoat and another fashionable bag big enough to hold a bowling ball. The doorman took the opportunity to grin at Rake, and then opened the door to Helene, saying some shitty pleasantry that he'd delivered well in his hiring interview. Helene smiled distractedly at the doorman and then looked up to see Rake.

She smiled genuinely.

Rake's smile was an echo and then he was taking her arm and leading her across the lobby, now perfectly at ease, as if his ten minutes of pacing was nothing but a forgotten memory. Neither spoke. For Rake's part, it was as if to speak would ruin it all, make Helene nothing more real than a character in a film.

That, and he didn't want to risk pissing her off yet.

They entered the lift and she smiled at him again confidently. "Hello, Rake."

"Hi."

He waited. The lift dinged and he led her to his flat, opening the door for her. She entered, turned and smiled. "Did I disturb anything important?"

He shook his head. "Just work."

She nodded, uninterested, and turned to look out over the city. He watched her, noticing her inclining her head down.

"It looks so pretty from up here. All the lights, the colours. Remember, we could just about see all this from the park in Plumstead."

"A better view from here," said Rake.

"I would once have said the view was better from my house—y'know, a private garden and all that, sculpted trees—but now I think I agree with you, a better view from here."

She turned then. Her smile was hesitant, unsure.

"You, er, had dinner?" he asked. "We could get some food?"

She shook her head—"I'm not hungry"—and started to take off her coat. She was wearing a knee-length deep-red dress, fitted enough that he appreciated it, demure enough for work. He took her coat from her, then folded it over the back of the La-Z-Boy.

"A drink?"

She sighed and then nodded. "It might help." She seemed to be waiting for something.

He turned and fixed her a dirty martini, expertly letting only a little olive brine in. He was aware of her eyes on him. When he finished and looked up she was looking up the river to the city again. He walked up beside her and handed her the drink. She stared at the olive in it for a moment, but he suspected that was just because that was where her eyes had rested rather than she had any particular interest in it. She took a sip, concentrating, it seemed, entirely on the taste, then she closed her eyes and sighed.

"You OK?" Rake asked.

Helene stared at him then, allowing him to read her face, and then pulled on a false smile, brittle and bright.

"Come on, Helene, we're old friends, what's the matter?"

"You wanted to see me again, didn't you?"

"Of course."

She nodded. "I..."

Rake waited.

She drank the rest of the martini and then chewed on the olive. Rake regarded her over the glass as he sipped at his.

"Look, Helene, yes, I wanted to see you again, I've been thinking about you, you know? A lot." *A hell of a lot.*

"Ah. You didn't call."

"Neither did you."

She grinned at that. "It was your turn."

"I didn't think you wanted to hear from me."

"Neither did I."

"So what—"

She stepped forward, close to him. "No questions, Rake, not now."

And then she kissed him.

Helene was lying down and smoking, taking in deep drags and watching the clouds she breathed out hang in the air above the bed. Rake was propped up on one elbow, watching her, noticing how she seemed entirely absorbed in what she was doing, completely at ease.

She raised her left hand up, turning it from side to side. The engagement ring sparkled in the early-morning light.

"I suppose I should pawn this first. There's seven fucking grand right there."

Rake grinned. "You left him then?"

She nodded. "You were right, it was dead years ago, but the effort to split the assets—we bought that house together, you know, and then there was the furniture, the cutlery, the cars..."

"You were staying together for the cutlery?"

Her eyes slid over to Rake then. "It was just easier. As hard to split the house as to organise a fucking wedding."

"You wouldn't have married him."

She sighed then. "Years ago I might have. Who knows." She took in another deep drag and sighed it out. "You know, I think there was only one man I truly loved."

Rake felt a deep sick feeling slide into his gut. "Cezek?"

She laughed. "No, Jeez, no, I wasn't that stupid." Then she frowned. "No, Chad. He was my first and it was ever so terribly teenage, but it was love. Had he lived? Who knows, maybe it would have turned into ash, just like all the rest."

"Helene..." *What would telling her achieve?*

"What?"

Rake smiled. "Nothing."

She sat up, stubbing the cigarette out on an overflowing ashtray. "Well, are you going to offer me breakfast?"

Rake grinned. "If I do, will you stay and actually enjoy it?"

She inclined her head. "I might."

So Rake got up and started making toast, eggs and bacon. He didn't bother asking her if she wanted any, but he figured that she'd not refuse if it was in front of her. Helene showered and then padded through to the kitchen area and sat on the stool at the breakfast bar. Rake watched her. This time she was different—still Helene, still here, even if her hair was restyled back to perfect.

He smiled and passed over her breakfast.

"I didn't know you could cook."

He nodded. "Well, I had to learn."

She stared at it for a moment. He watched her, then decided to leave her whilst he finished making a cappuccino. He was happy to hear the sounds of a knife and fork against a plate. He handed her her drink and sat opposite her with his breakfast.

"I... I lost my job." Her eyes were shimmering.

"What?"

She spat the words out as if they were poisonous to her. "I lost my fucking job. All that work, all those hours, all that hard work, and they've just thrown me out on the fucking street." She shook her head, tears squeezing out at the corner of her eyes. "Shit, I mean shit."

Rake was up and around the breakfast bar, his arm around her. "It will be OK, Helene, you can get another job."

She laughed then. "Don't you get it? No one's spending, no one wants a management consultant when they're already firing their staff on their own. Fuck!"

"Oh."

"What am I going to do now? I'm fucking skint! Who knows when I'll work again."

"Come on, Helene, come on, it's not all that bad, you know? You still got all your investments—"

"Yeah, but I don't want to touch those. Not if I don't have to."

"And there are still people hiring."

She laughed. "Don't lie to me, Rake, I do know what it's like out there." She sighed. "Shit, I know loads of people who've lost their jobs, and I felt sorry for them, but kinda, I didn't really want to get too close, y'know? Stupid as it sounds. And I know all the lies. 'There are jobs out there.' 'The market's hit the bottom, it can only go up.' 'Now you can figure out what you really want to do.' 'At least you have time for the gym.' All that shit. I've said it myself, but it doesn't mean it's true." Rake said nothing. "I think the bottom's fallen out of the market, it's sinking and us with it."

"The housing market? Yeah."

"No, the fucking consultancy market. I suppose I knew it was too good to be true, those wages for practically nothing, I... fuck, why did I do this?"

"For Rich?" asked Rake, curious.

She eyed him then. "You think you understand me? You think you know? You've not even seen me for twelve fucking years, Rake."

"Come on, Helene, chill out. I'm sure you can find something good, with your skills..."

She sighed and got out a cigarette. Rake thought that was a good sign. Perhaps she'd at least smoke it before leaving.

"Maybe for Rich," she admitted after a few minutes of

silent contemplation. "I think that maybe he'd not want a wife who was a biologist on a fucking eleven-grand-a-year grant. It's embarrassing... but then..." She angrily fiddled with the lighter for a few minutes, until Rake lit her cigarette with his own before getting himself a smoke. "I don't know. Once you're in, you're in, you know? You get addicted to all that money, to having whatever the fuck you want." She sighed. "I used to think I didn't care about money, but God, was it tempting." She took a deep drag. "He's out on his ear as well."

"Who? Rich?"

She nodded. "I guess it's unfair. We've both been fired and then, in the fallout, I just, well, I left."

Rake nodded.

"I don't even know he's of the same opinion as me, if he thinks our relationship has been dead for years. I'd understand if he'd had an affair, but I really don't think he has."

"He know about me?"

She shrugged. "What does that matter?"

Rake raised his eyebrows and smoked.

"I don't know. Maybe, maybe not. I doubt he'd care." She sighed. "I should have left him a year ago. What was I doing?" She eyed him then. "You do know you weren't the first?"

"I had guessed."

"I mean, fuck... Still, I don't feel too bad. The fucker. You know what he said to me as I left?"

"What?"

"'I want the ring back.'" She laughed. "The fucking ring, can you believe it? I texted him to tell him I'd pitched it into the Thames or something suitably dramatic like that." She shook her head. "The fucking ring. That'll probably be about a year's rent on some dive flat..." And then she was sobbing.

Rake put his arm around her. He decided that the best thing to say, given the circumstances, was nothing. After all, he didn't think she'd want to hear how she now had all that time to spend at the gym.

She cried herself back together and then she was blowing her nose and fixing her eye make-up to complete the recovery. She smiled at Rake. "Thanks," she said. "For just being there, you know? It's been years and yet you're still... well, y'know."

Rake nodded. "Look, Helene, I'm sorry, you know? All those years ago, I don't think I left particularly well, and I don't think I said what I meant to say."

Her eyes were like hot coals. "Oh? What did you mean to say? Sorry I lied?"

Rake stared at her.

"I mailed Cezek back. He found me on Facebook... It turns out that you weren't entirely honest with me."

Rake's mouth dropped open.

"Yeah, I thought so. Shit, Rake, what the fuck were you up to when we were younger? Why did you make up that stupid story about Cezek?"

"Which stupid story?" asked Rake in a small voice.

She shook her head in exasperation. "How many did you make up?" Then she sighed and started packing her cigarettes back into her bag. "Not that it matters now. I don't mind that you broke me and Cezek up, but fuck me, with you gone, and me avoiding him, I had no one to hang around with until I went off to uni. It was horrible. Eight months of horrible."

"That... that I am sorry for, Helene. I think I could have left in a better way. I think we could have met up in London. I think at the time I was after a clean break, but maybe it might have been better if—"

"Oh, Rake, you're babbling." She slammed the catch on her handbag shut and stood up. "Look, it doesn't matter, OK? A lotta time down the drain since then."

"I did it for you, you know."

She tilted her head to the side and shrugged. "Maybe." Then she smiled. "I gotta go, really, now's not the time to pick over old bones." She kissed him on the cheek then and he pulled her in close for a proper kiss. She responded and then smiled. He showed her to the door.

"Don't be a stranger, Helene."

"I won't." She smiled, her hand on the door frame. "Thank you, Rake. Talking it all over with you has really helped me sort things out in my head. I think I can talk to Rich much more calmly now."

And then she blew Rake a kiss and was out in the corridor.

Fuck, thought Rake.

Obscene

1996: Who'da Thought It, Plumstead

Another Friday. Lacking both the money and the creativity to think of doing anything else, Rake headed to the pub. He had the remains of his twenty-quid rent money to spend. He could avoid his mother at least until Sunday, as Saturdays were spent working at the Co-op. She'd shown a little sympathy on account of him getting beaten up, and hadn't made too much of a fuss about the rent as of yet. But she would as soon as he pissed her off again, so he figured that would be much harder to do if he was out of the house.

So he strolled over to the pub. He saw Seth: outside, leaning up against a wall, smoking.

"What you doing out here? You been chucked out?" asked Rake.

Seth shook his head and gestured at the bar. "It makes me feel sick to watch. One of us should tell her."

"Who?"

"Helene. It's just obscene."

Rake peered through the window, but he could only see enough to realise that there were two people at their now-usual table in the corner.

"Fucking Chad was my mate." Seth squashed the rolled-up cardboard roach. "And this ain't right."

"I know." Rake couldn't think of anything else to say.

Seth shook his head. "One day, I'm gonna fucking tell her. She'll thank me, I reckon. She should know the fucking truth." He made to go into the pub and Rake grabbed his arm.

"You can't do that!"

Seth scowled at him. "Why the fuck not? We were conned into this. All this time we've been protecting that fucker. But if she cared at all for Chad, she oughta want to kill that fucker."

"Look, not Helene, OK? She can't know."

"Why the fuck not?"

Rake didn't know what to say, so led Seth up into the pub garden. For some reason he didn't want to be near the door. "Look, it'd destroy her. She's been through enough, and she cares for Cezek."

"She won't when she knows the truth."

"Just leave it, OK? Helene, she's delicate, like porcelain or some shit, she can't cope with that."

"Fucking porcelain? Fuck, Rake, you're a complete fucking idiot. I tell you what, you go in there and see if you can stomach it. It's making me feel ill."

Rake frowned. "OK, let's just go inside and see, and leave it, OK? No one's gonna say nothing today, OK?"

Seth scowled. "One day, that fucker's gonna get what he deserves."

Chad

1994: The Dip, Plumstead Common

It was only a few short months until their GCSE's and, even better, only a few short weeks until they were released from school to revise for the exams. Helene had been talking excitedly about finally burning her grey, grey and grey school uniform, as sixth formers got to wear black suits so they were easily mistakable for old enough to drink if they went to the pub at lunchtime.

The six of them from class 1-5 were still friends: Cezek, Rake, Helene, Stacie, Seth and Chad. They'd known each other since the first day of junior school, and Rake was pretty sure that he'd seen Helene up on the common before that, but she'd never been able to remember that meeting. They'd decided to stay friends in secondary school and it'd kinda worked, less because they were great friends and more because they all lived so close that they just bumped into each other the whole time.

Still, some of them were closer than that.

Rake wasn't sure exactly when Chad and Helene had started going out. It was a big secret for a while as Helene thought she'd get into trouble with her mother. Her mum turned out to be cool with it. Rake could see why. Chad was the sort of guy that mums ended up liking. He had charm and personality, he could pull a good cheeky-boy grin and magically get out of any trouble he was in—provided, of course, that he was in trouble with an older woman. That cheeky-boy grin helped to disguise his size. He was tall, six foot, but not lanky. He was starting to get broad across the shoulders and was going to grow up to look like he should play rugby.

It was a perfect, late-spring night, the air was clear and fresh with opportunities and it was a Friday. They had booze and smokes and were going to go down the common to enjoy them. That Thursday, however, Chad and Helene had been up to, well, who knew what up in the park and Helene had ended up rocking home at eleven pm. On a school night. And she was now grounded.

They knew this as Helene's sister, Marie, wasn't grounded and had been running down from Helene's house to the lake at the bottom of the common with various messages and comments. Thus far, there had been two angry messages for Chad, one general message and two apologetic reversals for Chad.

At eight pm it was finally Marie's bedtime and they could break out the skunk and Co-op own-brand vodka without fear of being told on. The lake at the bottom of the dip was a good place to get up to shit, cos the trees lined the top so no one could peer down and see what they were doing.

Seth rolled, liberally sprinkling in the skunk, and they smoked and drank vodka. Chad remarked that Helene would be pretty sore to have missed it. Cezek asked what the fuck they had been up to, but Chad was a gentleman and said nothing. He couldn't stop the smile that formed on his face though, and that smile became wider and wider as they smoked more that evening.

And then Chad thought it was a pretty good idea to skim some stones across the slimy water. Like everything that involved physical skill, Chad was naturally good, Rake was OK and Cezek was too rough and impatient. Seth couldn't be bothered to skim stones and instead sat on a rock, smoking, as if he was sunning himself. As it was a gibbous moon above, Rake supposed that he was, or as close as a goth would allow themselves to get.

They smoked some more, drank some more. Stacie got drunk enough to try flirting with Seth, which always freaked him out. The poor guy never knew quite what to do or how to get her to leave him alone.

Cezek, having found what he declared was the perfect skimming stone, said he was gonna skim it all the way across the pond. He made such a fuss about it. And then he tried. It bounced off the slimy water and then sank, leaving a hole in the oily surface. Chad laughed.

Cezek, pissed off, waded into the water to try and find it. He was bending over and dragging his fingers through the mud, saying it was the best skimming stone he'd ever seen.

Chad, laughing, went over to help him, getting into the water and bending over, the water above his elbows.

Rake never knew quite what happened next—whether Chad, still laughing, slipped, or Cezek kicked him under the water. There was a yelp of surprise as Chad landed with a splash, and they were all laughing and Cezek bent forward to help him up.

Then Rake realised there was something wrong. He picked it up at gut level first, before he realised that Cezek wasn't helping Chad up, but holding him under. Chad was bigger and stronger than Cezek, but, when needed, Cezek had a kind of crazy strength. And maybe Chad panicked. The guy couldn't swim.

Rake was running over, then wading, arms swinging wide as he dragged his feet through silt. Chad's eyes rolled like a barking dog's, he was thrashing at the water, and Cezek, Cezek was just pushing him under, saying nothing, watching Chad dispassionately.

Rake pulled at Cezek and then tried to pull Chad up out of the water, and then Seth was beside him, pulling at Chad too.

Cezek suddenly let go and stepped back, and Rake and Seth were pulling Chad out of the water, up onto the muddy bank. Chad's eyes were open and staring, creepy in the moonlight.

"What? What did you do?!" said Stacie.

"You know first aid, do something!" said Rake. She wasted precious seconds staring with her mouth hanging open and then crouched and started doing mouth-to-mouth and heart compressions or some shit.

Cezek sat on the rock where Seth had been sitting, dried his hands off on his jeans and lit a cigarette, watching them with flat eyes. The fucker still hadn't said a fucking thing.

"Come on, Chad, come on," said Seth, tapping Chad's hand.

"Is he dead then?" asked Cezek. He looked mildly curious.

"What the fuck have you done?" said Rake.

"I tried to pull him out, you all saw it."

They stopped. Stacie stopped with the mouth-to-mouth. Chad hadn't moved or responded in any way, so Rake figured that there was little point telling her to carry on. They were all staring at Cezek. He raised his eyebrows and calmly drew on his cigarette.

"You bastard! Why the fuck did you do that?" shouted Seth. Then he swung a wild punch at Cezek, who smartly punched Seth on the chin, knocking him back.

"No need to go crazy at me."

"I... I'm gonna call an ambulance!" said Stacie, and then she was running up out of the dip to the road.

Rake looked down at Chad. The guy's lips were whiteish blue. He didn't think an ambulance would help.

"You fucking bastard! Why did you kill him? Why?" asked Seth.

Cezek shrugged. "I didn't kill him. You did. You went fucking crazy and tried to drown him, and the fucker hit you on the chin as you did it." Seth went pale. "Isn't that right, Rake?"

"Fucking hell, Cezek, Seth ain't taking the rap for this."

Cezek smiled. "So maybe we all say he got drunk, decided to fuck around in the water, slipped and by the time we got to him..." Cezek spread his fingers out wide. Seth and Rake looked at each other.

Stacie ran back down. "Me mum's called an ambulance and everything!"

Cezek stubbed out his cigarette with his foot and then looked around at all of them. "If our stories don't match we're all going down for murder."

"Murder?" squeaked Stacie.

Cezek nodded. "Now if you all do what I say, we'll get out of this just fine."

"But I didn't murder anyone!" said Stacie.

Cezek nodded. "Neither did I." Rake stared at him. "I

just tried to save my friend."

"You fucker," said Seth. "You fucking planned to do this shit, all that crap with the fucking skimming stones."

Cezek snorted. "Course not. Don't be stupid."

There were blue and red flashing lights up on the road. They all looked up the dip. Cezek grinned at them all. "Just do what I said, and everything'll be fine." He shrugged at Chad. "It's too late for him anyway."

Then there was a circus of paramedics and coppers. Cezek explained the story. Stacie started wibbling about doing mouth-to-mouth. Rake saw Marie's pale face at the edge of the crowd, then she vanished.

The coppers asked them all what had happened. Seth and Rake looked at each other.

"I don't know, officer, I was over there," said Stacie, pointing at the bank. "I couldn't see nothing from there, it's well dark down here."

"He... slipped," said Seth. He shook his head and looked down. "The poor fucker, he couldn't fucking swim..." Seth looked up beseechingly. "Me an' Rake tried to get there in time..."

Rake just nodded.

Then there was a shout and Helene squeezed through the gap in the fence, as quick as a cat or a cat burglar. She was still in her school uniform as she padded past him. She saw Chad and screamed. She sprinted over to him, but a copper tried to lead her away, so she turned and ran over to them.

"Is he... is he dead?" she asked Rake.

Rake and Seth looked at each other, and then Rake nodded.

Rake hoped he would never again see anyone look like Helene looked at that moment.

And then Cezek was there beside her, and he put his hands, the hands he'd drowned Chad with, on her arms and then Helene turned and just wept on him and Seth was looking at this scene in horror, the horror Rake felt pretty sure was reflected in his own face.

And Cezek looked over at Chad with something like a smirk.

Then Helene's mother arrived, following Helene's sister, and Helene ran to her and just wept. "He's dead, Mum, they say he's dead."

And Rake wondered what the point of the truth would be.

Descent

2008 - A Bar in Soho

Cezek was worried, rightfully so. He'd called Rake and summoned him to a bar. Rake would have told Cezek to fuck right off, except he was curious as to how much trouble the fucker was in. By Rake's guess, a lot. Cezek stood to lose about half of his empire.

The thought made him smile and there wasn't that much to smile about these days.

So he turned up at the bar. It was trashy-classy, the sort of place people went to flash their cash. And, like everywhere people went to flash their cash these days, it was either full of rich people with government bonds who were discreetly trying to enjoy it, or those in denial.

Cezek looked bad. His pink wide-boy tie was partially unknotted, but not as if some dancer had undone it for him, as if he'd fiddled with it himself. He smelt strongly of cigarettes, his hair was a mess and he was slumped over the table with three empty cocktail glasses in front of him.

Rake smiled. Nothing like a bit of schadenfreude.

"You all right, Cezek, me old china?"

"All right? You think I could be fucking all right?"

Rake sat down. A cocktail waitress came and took his order. He noticed she kept her distance from Cezek and his mind wrote all sorts of stories about what had happened before he got here, but maybe she just didn't want to get too close to desperation. She smiled at Rake, briefly, a professional smile, not the grin of someone after the lifestyle. She looked like there weren't many people for her to try her I'll-marry-you-for-ten-mil routine on.

She trotted off and returned with a Long Island iced tea, extra gin, please.

"Fuck, I don't understand this at all. Everyone knows that houses only go up in value, it's like the fucking law of the universe, everyone knows it."

Rake decided that Cezek didn't need a lesson in over-valued asset prices.

"Safe as houses, safe as fucking houses. You buy one, do it up, sell it, take the profit and buy another, then start renting them out and using that money to buy another... Shit, I ain't got hardly any empty houses and I'm still losing money and my renters are asking for a fucking discount!"

"So sell."

"Sell? At these prices? Are you a nutjob? No, I just gotta hold out until the market bounces back. It'll bounce back, right? It always does. Law of the fucking universe."

Rake nodded. "Yeah, we've definitely hit the bottom now."

Cezek nodded. "I hope so, I fucking hope so, cause I can't take too much longer of this shit. I'll lose everything."

"What do you mean?"

Cezek shrugged. "Well, dodgy accounting, you know? Certain companies owning the same assets as others." He shrugged. "All legit, y'know? Well, almost, but if it comes out that I ain't got quite as much as people think I got... well, fuck knows... it ain't good."

Rake nodded. "So how much—"

"Don't even fucking ask, Rake, OK? I'm only telling you on account of us being old mates, that and you don't work in property."

Rake nodded and decided to pass the information on to Big Phil, who did.

"How about you? You all right? Not scared like some of them pussies?"

Rake gulped most of his drink. The gin stung his mouth and then sang in his head. "I'm fine, fucking fine. They've already laid off all the people they're gonna lay off." He finished off the last gulp of the cocktail. "Removing some of the dead weight, y'know? But I'm good, so fucking good, I'll probably be on an even bigger bonus this Christmas."

Cezek scowled, looking envious, and Rake decided that he'd tell Big Phil to discreetly pull out of everyone who owed money to Cezek.

"Fucking A. Well, when the market picks up, I'll shift some of my dead-weight houses. I gotta couple of flats that don't seem to get tenants... looked like a nice fucking area too. Woolwich, right next to the council estate for them fuckers that win the pools." He laughed then.

Rake waved his glass at the cocktail waitress.

"You, er, you hear anything from Helene?" asked Rake, not even admitting to himself that that was why he had come here.

Cezek stared at him then. His frown softened into a smile. "Yeah, she takes a long fucking time to reply to an email, she does. The last one I sent about a week ago and she's still not replied. I thought management consultants were big on their emails, checking their fucking Blackberries during sex or some shit—but not Helene, of course. Fucking strange to think of her doing that job. She never seemed the type to get off on bossing people around."

"Yeah."

"That fucking Seth, though, she said some fucker'd told her some shit about me, she was all aggressive, telling me to leave her alone, and I fucking ask, 'why?' and that's when I hear all this shit that cunt's been saying about me."

"Oh." The waitress returned. Rake gave her a fifty as a tip, absent-mindedly as if it were still 2006. She flashed a hundred-grand-grin at him then, but he was largely oblivious.

"I tell her it's all complete bollocks, y'know? All this shit about stuff we'd done when we were younger, it was just cos of that she said she didn't want to hear from me."

"She... want to hear from you now?" asked Rake.

Cezek nodded. "Course she does, why wouldn't she? I think she's in Paris or some shit, so just as soon as she bothers replying to my email, I'll sort out meeting up with her when she gets back."

Rake was pretty sure she wasn't in Paris.

Probably in Notting Hill, patching up her fucking relationship.

He gulped another half of the cocktail and wondered why he bothered ordering one of the ones with ice-cubes.

"She didn't say it was Seth that told her that shit, she told me she'd just heard it round Plumstead, but I fucking know it was him. Fuck, I ain't even seen that cunt for five years an' he's still managing to make trouble."

"It might not have been Seth. People gossip in Plumstead."

Cezek shook his head. "Nah, I fucking know it was that cunt."

Lies

1996: Plumstead Common

Helene was smoking, watching the city, perched up on the steps of the running machine, her back to the dip on the common. Rake jogged over. "Your mum know you come over here to smoke?" he asked, startling her.

She grinned and shook her head. "I told her I'm stressed on account of my coursework or some shit, that I'm taking a walk, an' it's a lot less stressful to sit up here and smoke than crane my ears for her sneaking up the stairs." She tilted her head to the side. "What you doing?"

Rake was wearing jogging bottoms, trainers, a long-sleeved t-shirt and fingerless gloves. "I'm exercising, ain't I?"

She raised her eyebrows. "Up here?"

"That's what it's for."

She looked at the post next to the steps as if seeing it for the first time. "It says you gotta run over this, then do fifty star jumps."

"What? I thought it was twenty."

And she was giggling.

Rake sighed, climbed up and sat down on the steps. "Can I have a smoke?"

She handed him the packet. He put one in his mouth and one behind his ear. She noticed, but didn't seem to mind, that was how fucking happy she was.

"How's Cezek?" he asked, reaching for her lighter.

She grinned. "Fine, he's fine."

"I take it you're going out now?"

She nodded. "Yes, it's great." Then she frowned. "At least I think so..."

"Why, what's he done?" asked Rake, pulling on the cigarette. He suspected that it cancelled out the jog over.

"Well, nothing, it's all fine, it's just..." She chewed on her lip. "Do you think I'm kissable, Rake?"

He nearly dropped the cigarette into his lap. "Wha—? I mean, I can't—"

"Oh, I didn't mean for you!" She blushed then. "Shit, no, it's just that, well, Cezek doesn't ever seem to kiss me."

"You spend another night on his floor?"

She shook her head. "No, I slept in his bed this time, but all he did was kiss me and only the once..." She looked puzzled. "I don't get it at all, he acts different when he's on his own, y'know? Nicer, but somehow younger."

"Oh."

"But maybe, do you think he's a virgin?"

"Yes."

"But what about all those stories?"

"Helene, you really shouldn't believe any of Cezek's stories, the guy's a bullshitter."

"Oh. Maybe I should be patient."

"Don't sleep with him, Helene." Rake didn't even know he was going to say it until he did.

She stared at him. "What?"

"It's... It's kinda obscene."

"Obscene? What the fuck?"

"It's like..." There was something entirely wrong with the idea.

"It's like what? You can't just come out with something like that! What the fuck is all this about? First Seth, then you. What the fuck have you got against my boyfriend?"

"What about Chad?"

Helene frowned. "Look, Chad's dead, y'know? He wouldn't expect me to spend the rest of my life crying over him, would he? He wouldn't have if it were me that drowned."

"You wouldn't have drowned." *Cezek wouldn't have drowned Helene, would he?*

And then suddenly she was crying. "I don't understand. I'm happy. I want to be happy. Why the fuck aren't you guys happy for me?"

"Because, Helene..." Rake sighed and dropped the cigarette butt on the floor.

"You're all arseholes, that's what it is. Just jealous of Cezek and me, and I don't know why. You have that Lise bird, y'know? So why—"

"Helene, listen, I gotta tell you something."

"No, you listen. I've had enough of this shit. It's not fair." And she got up. Rake grabbed her arm and got her to sit back down.

"Please, calm down, OK?"

"Calm down?"

"Look, you gotta understand, Cezek's not a nice person, OK?"

She sighed and sat back down, slumping forward, her knees up, her shoulders high, as if she were an eagle.

"That's OK. I know that, but it's OK."

"No, you don't get it." Rake skimmed his eyes over the city below him, as if the grey skyscrapers could offer up a solution. "That night, when I was beat up so bad, y'know? That fucker was with me, an' I said I needed to go to hospital and he just left me in the road."

Her eyes were wide.

"That's why you couldn't find him, he was lying low, hiding out."

"He left you?"

"Yeah, an' then I staggered to your house an'..."

"Oh."

"He's selfish, cares only about himself."

Helene got out a cigarette and started rolling it around her mouth.

"But that's not all of it, y'know?"

She stared at him then, the cigarette stilled.

"He's... not quite right, y'know? I mean he's crazy. We..." Rake looked down at the slices of Thames between the buildings below, shimmering like knives. "We went out for a few drinks that night, and it wasn't Terry that beat me up the second time."

"Who then?"

"Well, as we were walking home, Cezek sees this guy and for no reason whatsoever, just started hitting him with a bit of wood, y'know? Just on a whim or something. An' the guy was on the floor, passed out, his head smashed in and his nose broken, and Cezek looked like he was gonna carry on, just smashing the guy's head until he killed him."

Her mouth opened and she dropped the cigarette. "Did he?" she whispered.

Rake shook his head. "I stopped him, but he was going

crazy and as I pulled him away he thumped me in the ribs, breaking them."

"He did that to you?"

"Yes?"

"He put you in the hospital? Why the hell would you still drink with him?"

"He... yes, he did it. Y'know? But it was mostly an accident, he didn't mean to hurt me. He just went crazy at that guy and would'a killed him, just like that, as if it were nothing."

Helene was watching the smoke from the factories on the river turning into clouds.

"Y'see? That's the sort of person he is, crazy. An' if you stay with him, one day it'll be you." She turned to look at him then. "You understand that, don't you?"

She shook her head, pulled out another cigarette, dipping her head low so he couldn't see her eyes as she lit it. When she lifted her head as she exhaled Rake felt like a shit. "I... I just don't believe it." She said it in a tone of voice that made him think that she did.

"I'm sorry, Helene, that's why I wanted you to give up on him. I didn't want you to know what he was really like... but if you really want to date him, well, you shouldn't, because he's a fucking shit and you deserve better than that."

She lowered her head, looking at her fingers louchely holding the cigarette. "You an' Seth cooked this up together, did you?"

Rake shook his head. "What did Seth say to you?"

She shrugged. "I don't really know. He didn't make much sense. But he said I shouldn't see Cezek any more. He kept saying Chad was my mate, an', y'know, I know that, I do, but surely he doesn't expect me to never have another boyfriend just cos Chad died? That's not fair."

Rake didn't know what to say.

"An' you, is this story really true?"

Rake nodded enthusiastically. "You said Cezek is different when it's just you two. Maybe he is, cos he's different when you're not there as well. He's nastier, crazier. He does fucking stupid things for no reason." Rake ran his hand over his hair. "Shit, Helene, before you two were dating he was burning you and slapping you and spiking your drink and all that shit, what the fuck do you think will happen if you get more serious? How long before he freaks out and puts you in hospital?"

She bowed her head. "I... I dunno, Rake."

"You get it, don't you? That's what will happen to you, it's inevitable... An' if you sleep with him, well, he'll think it's OK, he'll think you're his, y'know, his fucking property, that's how it works with him."

"Guys aren't like that."

"Cezek is. He wants everything anyone else has. Once he gets it, he don't give a fuck about it no more, that's why..." Rake turned and looked down at the dip. *Was that why? Was Seth right? Had Cezek actually planned it all out?*

Nah... It had been a whim.

Helene had her fingers in her hair. "I don't want to be hit again," she muttered. Then she stared at Rake, imploring him with her eyes. "Is it my fault? Is this why guys are like this to me? Did I do something wrong?"

"What? What the fuck you talking about?"

"People wanting to hit me. I mean, I know Cezek did before, but I thought that maybe he won't no more..."

"What? Who else hit you? Surely not Chad?"

"No, he wouldn't have."

"Then who?"

She shook her head. Rake made to grab her hand, but then pulled his fingers away. Helene was staring at him.

"Who?" he asked.

"Me mum's old boyfriend," she muttered.

"Oh. What did he do?"

She sighed. "Look, nothing, OK? It's nothing."

And then she was up and running off back towards her house.

Rake realised he'd never seen Helene run before.

Lady in Red

Christmas Eve, 1996: Plumstead Common Working Men's Club

Rake hated Christmas. He was seventeen years old now, and he still had to spend Christmas Eve with his family.

They were all tip-toeing around on broken glass to try and keep their mum happy. She'd wrapped the presents and tidied the place up and even pre-cooked the fucking turkey. At five o'clock they'd had some sort of dinner, whatever was quick to make after making turkey, and then at six on the dot his old man started whingeing about getting down the Working Men's Club. His sister Amy and brother Geoff were ready to go, but his mum made a fuss about getting ready and it occurred to Rake that she always managed to get out of the house on time when she wanted to go somewhere. His father mentioned something similar and then they were delayed for twenty minutes more so they could argue about fucking turkeys.

No one even liked turkey.

Then they were off round the corner to the club. Rake hated the place. It was boring and just full of people trying to drink away the time at cheap club prices. A large proportion of his childhood had been spent here, bored shitless, drinking Pepsi sold in two-litre bottles, enough for an entire family.

Still, it wasn't as bad as it could have been. There were other people he knew who were there and bored shitless. They wandered in to the back room, where kids were more accepted and they usually put some live music act on. It had fake pine walls, red bucket seats, and tiny tables with a bin underneath for the disposal of scratch cards or bingo cards or whatever. The main decor was some awful schmaltzy Victorian paintings of a blonde six-year-old girl and her big blond dog. The same tacky plasticy decorations hung up here as they had in the pubs—they must have been cheap down Woolwich Market this year or something, and they just served to make the place look even more depressing.

His family sat down next to Stacie's. She was there, spruced up in some sequinned BHS rags. Stacie's mum was chatting away to Helene's mum—Stacie's dad usually signed them in to the damned place, cos women weren't allowed in by themselves, not even if the working man of the family had died. Cezek and Helene were sitting at the next table along, making that half of the room seem too small for anyone else. Seth wasn't there. His mum didn't socialise down the club.

Rake went up to the bar with his dad, who had decided that Rake was now old enough to be bought a pint of proper beer, rather than Fosters shandy. As he walked back past Helene, she glanced up at him. Her eyes skimmed over him as if he wasn't there, and then returned to Cezek. They were sitting close, very close. Rake noticed that their hands were resting about a centimetre away from each other on the seat between them. And they didn't move them.

It was odd. If they were going out, why the fuck couldn't Cezek bring himself to hold her hand?

"Come on, son, no need to take all fucking night over it," said his dad. Rake walked and sat down with his family. The first couple of drinks they all sat with their families—'cept Cezek of course, his mum was on the other side of the club with her boyfriend, someone Cezek hated. In Rake's case, he was stuck with his family because his mum had big ideas about family harmony, which meant that he had to ignore his friends. Still, it wasn't all that bad. His dad drank quickly and, having decided that Rake was now old enough to get served, sent Rake up to get the beers. Rake got himself one each time. His old man seemed happy enough after about five pints that Rake was able to half-inch a good chunk of the old man's baccy and divest it into his own packet.

Eventually, Stacie went and took up their usual position by the quiz machine. She stood there looking lonely. Cezek and Helene had fucked off somewhere, presumably to grab a quick smoke away from Helene's mum. Rake got the next round in, then scarpered, his mum having had enough gin and tonics to have forgotten about family harmony and that shit. The kids had also escaped and were running around the dance floor, getting in the way of the band—a guy and a girl with a keyboard, mic, guitar and backing tracks machine—setting up.

"Merry Christmas and all that shit," said Rake to Stacie.

"What you think they're doing out there?" She nodded to the door that Helene and Cezek had wandered off through. "It's fucking freezing."

Rake shrugged. He suspected that they were hiding

out in the snooker hall, rather than outside.

"You could go an' get them."

Rake shook his head and rolled himself a ciggie. "No fucking way."

"But it's boring here otherwise."

"Always boring in this fucking place. Like purgatory, we all gotta stick it out 'til last orders."

"What, to get to Christmas?"

Rake nodded. "An' we'll be back here for the two hours it opens on Christmas Day." Then his dad would be too drunk to eat the turkey, and there'd be a fight. It happened every year and Rake wondered why the fuck his mum didn't schedule the main meal for five pm rather than three, which would give his dad sometime to sleep it off.

"Gaaw, you're fucking Scrooge, in't ya?" At that point the band wibbled over the microphone about playing 60s, 70s and 80s music and started playing *Buttercup*. "Me mum says Helene's mum don't like Cezek."

Rake nodded.

"She said she'd rather Helene didn't date than go out with him!"

"She tell Helene that?"

Stacie rolled her eyes. "I doubt it. But Helene seems happy."

"You don't think it's..."

"What?"

"Well... obscene?"

"Obscene? What the fuck's that mean?" It seemed like the only word that did it justice. It was a shame that Stacie lacked the vocabulary.

"Wrong, it means wrong." Rake shook his head and lit his roll-up.

Stacie shrugged. "Fuck knows. She's stopped blanking me though."

He shrugged.

"I never thought they'd actually ever get it together. What do you think about it?"

"Where's Gary anyway?" asked Rake. He didn't really care for the fucker, but he wanted to stop discussing Helene.

"With his family, of course." Stacie grinned. "He's popping in on Christmas Day though."

Rake's dad was waving a fiver at him, and, like a good waiter, Rake went to the bar. He returned with a beer for him and one for his dad, and pocketed the change. His brother had been sent to get food, as there were a few packets of Mini Cheddars, some pickled onions and chunks of Cheddar cheese on the table. That was what passed as pub food in Plumstead, at least until the fish man came round with peppered and vinegared prawns and cockles.

When he came back, Helene and Cezek were up at the quiz machine. Helene was pulling on Cezek's arm. "Come on, come dance with me."

Cezek laughed. "I don't dance."

"Come ooooon..." She looked out over the floor. There were a few couples, loads of kids bouncing up and down and a few teenage girls in a posse dancing around an invisible handbag. "Don't you want to dance with me?" She looked genuinely upset. The band started playing *Lady in Red*. She smiled. "Come on, I'm even wearing a red dress."

"Look, Helene, I don't fucking dance for no one, got it?"

She stuck her bottom lip out and looked sulky.

"Dance with your sister if you want to fucking dance."

Cezek pointed at the gaggle of girls.

"You can't dance with your sister to this!" said Rake. Then he slammed down what was left of his eighth beer. "Come on," he said to Helene and led her to the floor.

Later Rake realised that he must have been very pissed, as there was no way he would have been seen dead dancing to Seb de fucking Burgh under normal circumstances.

But at the time, he didn't really give a fuck about embarrassment, and kinda jerked along to the music. Helene could dance. She looked happy and grinned at him, then looked over her shoulder at Cezek. He was scowling, no surprise there. As Helene could dance so well, and was wearing a tight red dress, Rake decided to go for broke and take her hand and spin her around a bit. It was a kinda drunken polka rather than anything else. Rake stopped spinning Helene. The room didn't stop spinning around him, and he grasped onto her for support.

"Rake, you OK?" She was staring up at him.

He nodded. And then tried to do one of those underarm spin thingies. It didn't quite work, but no one fell over so Rake decided to chalk it up as a win. And cos he was sooooo drunk, he sang, " 'Lady in red is dancing with me.' "

Helene giggled. "You're completely pissed."

" 'Cheek to cheek.' " Rake felt himself moving backward. Perhaps the club was sinking. Then he registered someone's hand was on his shoulder, pulling him away. He turned, saw Cezek's ugly mug and then Cezek's fist drove into his nose. Rake slumped backwards, but Cezek held onto him and punched him there again before letting Rake slump to the floor.

"Cezek!" screamed Helene. The music stopped and

Rake blinked at the ceiling, tobacco-stained white paint and red and gold foil decorations pulsing with the disco lights.

There was a smash of glasses. Rake lifted his head up to see what was going on and Cezek whacked him on the nose with one of those fucking pine tables.

Helene was still screaming and Rake looked up to see Cezek raising the table above his head. His eyes were bizarrely calm and he was looking at Rake as if he were nothing but an abandoned tire or dead fox. Then he brought the table down. Rake put his hands up to defend him, getting nothing worse than bruises.

Cezek lifted the table up again. People were shouting, but Cezek wasn't making any noise at all. As Cezek brought the table down Rake realised the fucker was going to keep doing that until he was dead. Rake half-stood and put his hands up, getting the edge of the table on his temple for his troubles. His vision wavered, he slumped forward and did his best to hold on to reality. When he could see again he realised he was on all fours.

Rake took a minute to gulp down the vomit that he could feel at the back of his throat. Then there was a thud. It didn't hurt, but his head felt like it was encased in cotton wool. He couldn't hear anything and just had the feeling of tipping forward like he was trying to learn to dive off the edge of a pool.

Reprise

August 2008: Rake's Penthouse, Poplar

Rake had left messages, on her phone, on her fucking work number—though he doubted she still used it—even with her mother, although he didn't explain why he was after Helene, but he got nothing. He almost called Cezek up for a drink to see if Cezek had any more useful information about Helene, but Rake decided to leave it. If her mum didn't know where the fuck she was, Cezek certainly wouldn't.

Shit.

Everything was feeling pretty shit. Outside it was hot, a fucking heatwave and all the girls were in almost see-through flowing dresses or little shorts and what was he doing? Musing over the fact he was nothing but a comfort fuck for Helene.

Fuck.

And work wasn't fun either. The last round of redund-ancies had lit a fire under everyone's arses. No one had money to spend on benders and they were all putting in the hours, Rake especially. He reckoned that work, like markets, had its own rhythm—a time to go on benders and a time to kill those hours. But it was depressing. The movie industry was OK, there was loads of wibbling about 3-D technology again, but there were some people talking about impossible things: runs on banks, the financial system breaking, countries going bankrupt. Bollocks, of course, but all rather depressing nonetheless.

And cos Rake was working so fucking hard, he missed her call.

When he noticed that, he called her back, not caring that it was five to midnight.

"Hi, Helene."

"Hi, Rake, I heard you were trying to get hold of me."

He sighed, perhaps too loudly, as he reckoned that the phone picked it up.

"OK, then, maybe you weren't."

"Hold on, Helene." He reckoned there was a good chance she was about to hang up on him.

"What?"

"Yes, I was trying to get hold of you. Were you just planning to leave it like that and go running back to Rich and not even tell me?"

"What? No, I've left Rich, you know that."

"Well, where are you living now?"

"I'm renting a flat."

"Can I come over?"

"It's a very cheap flat, Rake. I'm still job hunting."

"I don't care."

And then it was she who was sighing down the phone. "I can come to you, if you want."

"Yeah."

"OK, I'll be there in twenty."

She took thirty. When she arrived she was holding a large overnight bag. Rake grinned.

"You moving in?"

She just stared. Then she looked at the bag in her hand as if she was seeing it for the first time. "No, I came straight from Stansted."

"Oh."

He let her into the flat and she slumped into the La-Z-Boy. "God, I hate getting the last flight, if it's delayed the coffee shops aren't even open."

"Is that where you've been all this time? Abroad?"

She raised her eyebrow at him and then sighed. "Not quite. I moved out, got a fucking bedsit somewhere, y'know? But I'd arranged to go to a friend's hen party. Saturday night on the tiles, Sunday in a spa, that sort of thing."

Rake was just standing up, staring at her. Helene smiled at him.

"You think I could have a coffee?"

"Ah, yeah." Then he was fucking around with the machine. She kicked off her shoes and stretched her legs out. When he looked over he caught her massaging her temples. The machine finished its final steam explosion and he handed her a cappuccino.

"Thanks." She delicately sipped at the foam. "I thought about not going to the hen party. I wasn't in the mood at all."

He sat down on the chair opposite her.

"But I figured I'd already paid for it, I wouldn't get that money back." She smiled. "Then I thought, fuck it, and extended my stay at the spa for a week, took some time to do a stock-take, y'know?"

"And, er, what did you think?"

She examined the coffee foam for a minute. "Were you serious? About moving in?" She looked up.

Rake smiled. "If you want to."

She sort of stared off into the distance. "It's moving kinda fast, isn't it?"

Then he was over there, perching on the edge of her chair, putting his arm around her. "Is it? Don't you think you've been guilty of moving too slow? I mean with leaving Rich."

She stared at him. "I... I suppose so."

"So stay. It's cool, I'd love to have you. I'm working quite hard at the moment, but you can have the run of the place, do job searches here, I got internet."

She smiled.

"So you'll stay?"

"At least for tonight."

Brandy and Blood

Still Christmas Eve, 1996: Plumstead Common Working Men's Club

His eyes were open, he knew that much, but the scene didn't make any sense. It was just colours and light, pulsing in time with the sick feeling in his stomach and the throbbing from his nose.

He blinked a little—not too much, as it hurt. He could hear noise, the repetitive tinny drumming, people, many people talking, shouting, then an orangey blob obscured the lights.

"Are you OK?"

He stared at a face that seemed to have no meaning, and then he realised that he was staring at Marie in her tan-coloured foundation that didn't match her skin-tone.

He sat up and looked around. Cezek had been dragged off to the edge of the dance floor by Rake's dad, Stacie's dad and a couple of nearby blokes, and they were doing their best to hold him there. Cezek's mum was peering over their shoulders, saying something soothing, no doubt. The band had stopped playing, but hadn't thought to stop the backing track, so the slow drum beat was just ticking on like an old-fashioned cartoon bomb.

Too many people were staring at him, so Rake gingerly touched his nose—it wobbled in a way noses weren't supposed to, causing more nausea—and then looked over at Cezek.

"He didn't mean anything by it, Cezek," Helene was pleading.

"Whore," spat Cezek. "You fucking whore!"

And she started sobbing, but she was looking at Rake.

Rake tried to get up and spat blood. He looked down. There was blood all over his face, down his top, on his best fucking jeans. He touched the back of his head and wasn't surprised that his fingers came away wet. His nose throbbed and he reckoned that it would hurt like hell when the beer anaesthetic wore off. When he glanced round, he realised everyone in the room was staring.

And then his mum was beside him, cradling his head and cleaning off the blood with a festive paper serviette covered in Mini Cheddar crumbs.

"Let go of me, you fuckers!" shouted Cezek, pulling against his captor. They held his arms out to either side, so he had to struggle like he was hanging on a cross.

"You need to calm down now, Cezek," said Rake's dad. "Just cool it."

"I'm calm, OK, now get your hands the fuck off me!"

Rake stood, expecting Cezek to come storming over to him. He watched the guy as if he were a fucking snake. His mum was left crouching there, holding the bloody serviette, as a reddened cheese crumb fell from it onto the carpet.

Cezek didn't move towards him, just jabbed at the air. "You're a fucker, Rake. You got your own fucking woman, so keep your dirty hands off've mine."

"Jeeez, I was only dancing." Rake hiccupped and felt the burning vomit in the back of his throat again. He had a horrible feeling he was going to blow chunks all over the dance floor and if that happened, he wouldn't be surprised if his nose hit the fake pine too.

"Yeah, an' who the fuck said you could dance with Helene?"

Rake was wobbling a little on his feet, but a rush of anger straightened his spine. "You're a cunt, Cezek, a right fucking cunt. You want a fight, short-arse? Come here and have one. You fucking sneak up on someone and hide behind a table!"

Rake's dad and the other heavies hovered near Cezek, ready to grab him.

Cezek looked around the room as if noticing it for the first time. He narrowed his eyes at Rake. "I think I made my fucking point." He made to move and Stacie's dad put his hand on his arm. "Get your fucking hand off me!"

Stacie's dad moved his hand, quickly, as if the evening's drinks hadn't been drunk at all.

"You better not start anything." But he said it to Cezek's retreating back and it came off as faked bravado.

Cezek stalked over to his seat and sat, folding his arms, and scowled, somehow meeting no one's eye, but taking in the entire room. No one moved, and then Helene trotted over and sat next to him. Once they started arguing, everyone seemed to relax and the band remembered to turn off the backing track.

Most people sat back down. Rake's dad walked over. "I think we'd better go, don't you, son?"

Rake looked around the room. No one would meet his eye except Marie, who grinned at him and whispered, "I think you're very brave," before his mother tutted and shooed her off.

"Let's go," his mother whispered. It was a whisper with a steel core.

The minor sideshow of his mother shouting at his brother and sister, who refused to be rounded up, was drowned out by the band starting up with fucking *Bridge Over Troubled Water*. They didn't mention anything, not even when the fifteen-year-old glass collector turned up to remove the table and mop down the dance floor.

His mother led the way, her back straight, her head held high, eyes locked forward as if she were walking to a guillotine. His dad exchanged a look with Stacie's, and both paused by Rake as he approached Cezek. Helene dropped her eyes as Rake walked past, as if he were a fucking hearse or some shit. Cezek gave him an evil look and seemed unaware that Rake and Stacie's dad were both watching him, ready to weigh in if things went wrong. Then Rake was past Cezek, past Helene, past the quiz machine, where Stacie was standing with her mouth open.

Then they were through into the main bar. The swing doors even banged behind them like it was a Western. A couple of the old boys that sat in the front bar started with shock when they saw him. One of the committee waddled over.

"You don't have to go, I'm gonna kick him out."

Rake's dad sighed. "I think I gotta take care of my son, clean him up." He shook his head. "He's a bad one, that one." Rake wasn't sure who his dad was talking about. "And I'd leave that fucker there, if I were you, not worth the aggravation."

"Well, we can't do that..." He looked unsure. "Still, it's not against the rules, exactly. It might be a committee matter. I think we might have to meet..."

Rake's dad shrugged and they walked out of the club into the cold. The icy air sobered Rake up a little and he started to feel very fucking sorry for himself.

They walked home in silence—well, other than his brother and sister who quarrelled and got shouted at by his mother.

Rake sat on the sofa, staring at the tree and the presents as his mum dabbed TCP over him.

His dad lit a saggy roll-up and decided to dispense some fatherly wisdom. "Sometimes, Seb, a wise man walks away. It don't mean he's any less of a man, but some things ain't worth it."

Rake wondered if his nose was broken. *Could they fix that crap by putting it in bandages?*

"An' really, a wise man don't hit on other people's girls."

"I wasn't hitting on her. I don't know what the fuck I was doing, I don't even like dancing, but I wasn't hitting on her."

"You just thought it would be fun to get into a fight, did you?" asked his mother. She seemed to think that wounds were cleaned the same way you rolled out pastry and his face throbbed worse with every touch.

"Mum, I'm clean, OK, leave it."

She slammed the kitchen roll down on the side table. "You don't care at ALL what I do for you! I'm just trying to clean up my THUG of a son, who EMBARRASSES me in front of all of my friends. Do you even CARE how I felt walking out of that room with everyone staring? They'll all be gossiping now. How will I EVER show my face there again?"

"Come on, it's not my fault that Cezek went off on one,

is it? It wasn't even a fair fight, the fucker hit me with a fucking table! What am I supposed to do? Say, oh Cezek, me fucking china, don't attack me from behind, it might embarrass me mum!"

"No one's going to think any less of you, dear," said his dad to his mum. "Everyone remembers what being seventeen is like. By tomorrow everyone will have forgotten and be talking about some other shit."

His mum shook her head angrily. "It doesn't work like that, they'll be talking about this for weeks, saying I'm a bad mother—"

"Mum, it has nothing to do with you, OK? Everyone will blame me, not you, and anyway, it's all Cezek's fault, and you're not his mum."

His mother squeezed out some tears, then dabbed at her eyes with the TCP-covered tissue, then contorted her face up in pain as real tears started to flow. She ran out to the kitchen, his dad ran after her and then Rake heard water running. He picked up the tissue and the TCP and started, very gingerly, dabbing at his nose.

After about five minutes, his mum came back in, her eyes red and raw. "Well, Sebastian, you've ruined Christmas, I hope you're happy." Then she stalked off upstairs and the door slammed.

His dad looked up at the ceiling for a moment, then left and returned with two brandies. He put one in front of Rake.

"It ain't all that bad," he said, pointing at Rake's nose. "Looks worse than it is, I reckon." His dad wasn't all that good at lying. He gulped his brandy down in two swallows. "Yeah, it ain't all that bad."

Then he headed up to bed.

Rake looked in the mirror. Two black eyes already

forming, a nose that was three times its usual size, cuts and fucking splinters to pick out of his head and arms and when he breathed deeply he still had the pain from the broken ribs from the last time he got beat up. He dabbed TCP on everything that hurt, trying not to remember how much better Helene had been at that job.

Then he sipped his brandy before going to bed.

He was pretty sure his nose was broken.

Choices

2008: Rake's Penthouse, Poplar

The next day at work, Rake was only a part-timer, his mind only half on the job. As soon as reasonable, he scarpered for the day, not caring in the slightest about markets or finance or the financio-apocalypse—some of the guys in the office were using that word, only semi-ironically.

He rushed home, expecting an empty flat, hoping he was wrong. He was too impatient to wait for the lift, so he ran up the stairs until, panting, he stopped at the fifth floor. Too stubborn to admit he was a long time from gym fodder, he walked up the remaining eight flights. He paused at the top and let his breathing slow a bit whilst he smoothed down his hair. Then, as if it were completely casual, he unlocked the flat.

Helene was sat on the floor, piles of paper spread out in front of her, her laptop on the coffee table, a pen in hand. It was odd seeing her in non-work clothes—she'd grown into the sort of woman who never really dressed down. She had a full face of make-up, hair perfect, and was wearing a patterned summer dress—not the floaty, hippy kind, the structured, tight, expensive kind. She tucked a stray hair behind her ear, and the engagement ring caught the light. She finally noticed him, looked up and smiled.

"Why do you wear that?"

She stared. "It's hot."

He frowned. "No, the ring, not the dress. I like the dress."

She looked confused, then looked at her hand and back to him, then nodded. "Ah, Rake, this has been nothing but a bit of jewellery to me for years." She held her hand out in front of her to look at it. "I guess, well, I want to remember that I once thought it was reasonable to wear seven grand on my finger." She chewed at her lip slightly. "I s'pose I want to get my money's worth from it before I pawn it. Before I'm officially poor."

Rake sighed and sat on the floor next to her. "You'll get a job, Helene, don't worry about that."

She sighed. "I don't know. I don't even know if I want to do consultancy anymore, but if I don't do that, what the fuck will I do?"

Rake smiled. "You could do anything. Management, accountancy, hell, even investment banking if you were willing to learn how."

She regarded the piles of paper. "Yeah, I've been looking at all that. I just..." She sighed. "I don't know if I could get the job. I think I've had enough of selling, even to get a job, you know? I just don't know if I can be bothered to paint on the bullshit... I know it's how the world works but..."

Rake sat down on the floor with her. "But what?"

"But I think I just want some truth, something fucking genuine. Everything in the City is hidden under layers of lies, obfuscation, vagueness, sales talk, no one ever says what they mean. I can play the game, y'know, know what's true and how to talk around it. I pity the poor fuckers that don't."

Then she was staring at an application. Rake took her hand and she looked at him.

"You could do something else, y'know, work in some other type of job."

"But what? What the fuck can I do? And what even pays half decent?"

"Biology? You could go back to school, get trained up as a biologist, that could be cool."

She rolled her eyes. "I'd be practically thirty-five before I even finished."

"But it was what you really wanted to do at school."

She shrugged. "I had a lot of stupid ideas when we were young. I knew nothing about how the world really works." She looked out over the city, talking to the skyline, not to him. "It's like I'm addicted now, you know? I could quit the drinking, forget the recreational drugs... I've never tried quitting smoking, don't know if I could or not to be honest." Rake frowned. "But it's like I'm addicted to the money now, y'know, and that's worse. Maybe if I'd never known it, if I'd always been poor, then yes, I could go back to school, but I'm used to the lifestyle now..."

She turned away from the window, fully present in the room once more. "But, of course, I can't get any fucking money unless I work for it."

Rake started to calculate how much money a woman like Helene would need to feel rich.

"Oh, don't look like that!" And she was holding his hands. "I'm just being maudlin, really, I s'pose. As long as

I'm out of Plumstead, I can count myself as a success."

"Seriously, Helene, I'm sure that there are plenty of jobs out there that you can do."

She smiled a plastic smile at him. "Yes, I guess something will come along..."

Missing The Party

New Year's Eve, 1996: Rake's House

Christmas was shit. Rake drank to drown the pain and grew two purple, puffy eyes. A week passed. He didn't see his friends. He didn't want to go to the pub and see Cezek, not until his injuries had healed up—he didn't want the fucker to know how bad he'd hurt him.

New Year's Eve was a bright sunny day, no snow to speak of, but cold and frosty so all the colours were washed out and painful. Then sunset and evening rolled around. Rake sulked. Even his mum didn't come any-where near him. Stacie was having a New Year's Eve party, and, cos his face wasn't healed up yet, he didn't want to go and give Cezek the satisfaction of seeing the damage he'd done.

He was gonna see 1997 in alone in front of the fucking TV.

There was a knock at the door. Rake was in too bad a mood to answer it, so his sister went and then came to get him. His dad gave him a significant look as Rake went to the door.

"Rake! Oh my God, look at you!" It was Helene,

dressed in a black and red velvet dress, leather trench-coat and lots of eyeliner. She had a deep bag with a plastic bag around a litre of Coke sticking out of the top.

"Yeah, look, let's walk." Rake's dad and sister were leaning round the door.

"Walk? You sure?"

"Yeah, come on."

She hesitated, and then nodded.

They left and walked off down the road.

"Can we... uh, can we walk up Bostall Woods?" Bostall Woods were perpendicular to the common, over the road, not even in Plumstead any more.

Rake shrugged. He didn't care where they went, he just wanted out of the house. It was boring and all his mum said was how terrible he was.

They wandered down from Plumstead and then up the huge tree-covered hill, talking vaguely about Christmas presents, but mostly sharing silences and cigarettes. They stopped at the top of the hill and sat on a dismembered and burnt tree, looking out over Plumstead.

"You all right?" she asked. "Your face..."

Rake shrugged.

"He woulda, wouldn't he?"

"Woulda what?"

She kicked at a few dry twigs, getting dirt on her high heels. "He would've killed you, wouldn't he? He wouldn't have stopped..."

Rake stared at some faded beer cans under dead twigs. "Maybe."

"If they hadn'ta pulled him off, he wouldn'ta stopped."

Rake frowned at Plumstead, squatting, a patch of small suburban houses arranged in rows upon rows on marching up the hillside. Some houses were blinged up in Christmas lights, most were nothing but yellow rectangles floating in nothingness like ships at sea.

"We were mates," muttered Rake.

"I can't believe it, I just can't believe it. It was awful. I thought he was going to kill you and I was screaming and he just didn't stop. I thought you were dead!"

Rake looked at her then. "I survived."

She started gnawing at her lip.

"You have a nice Christmas with him?"

She seemed to have mistaken her lip for pork scratchings.

"You see him?"

She nodded. "He... he was nice, real nice, real charming. He sauntered in on Christmas Day. I think me mum's scared of him, but he was really charming to her, grinning and smiling..." She sighed. "But we were both holding our breaths. y'know? Expecting... I don't know quite what."

"He was OK, then?"

"Yeah, yeah, he was OK." She pulled out another cigarette. The previous was still smouldering in the peaty mud at her feet. "Yeah, OK, just..."

"What?"

"I... I dunno, I think you were right."

He eyed her.

"About Cezek. It was just like you said, just like that. An' I think you're right, me mum's scared of him, y'know? How long til he's fucking beating me up like her boyfriend did her? I don't want that shit, I don't want it. I seen her make her mistakes, I don't want to make the same ones..." She sighed. "But sometimes, I feel like I'm fucking drowning, like I can't bloody breathe, an' I know I'm –"

"You tell him it's over?" She nodded. "Really?" Rake

was impressed. He hadn't thought that she actually would.

"He was mad. I came to warn you. He might come and try and beat you up again. I said it had nothing to do with you, but y'know..."

"Ah... that's why you wanted to come up here, rather than sit on the common."

She nodded and pulled a bottle out her bag. It was cheap own-brand Co-op vodka. "I got Coke too, and mince pies, no cups though, we'll just have to switch." She shrugged. "I thought we could at least see New Year's Eve in properly." She sniffed. "Cos Stacie's fucking invited Cezek to her party... I told her all about it, but..."

"You scarpered from the party?"

She nodded. "Do you want to go?" She opened the vodka. "I ain't gonna, but you can, if you want." She took a swallow and then made that strange gasping noise people do when they're not used to neat spirits.

"I wasn't gonna go."

"Good."

"You planning to sit up here all night?"

She shrugged and then grinned. "I got food, drink and even enough cigarettes to share them with you." She stuck her bottom lip out. "It's fucking New Year's Eve, I don't want to sit at home with me mum."

Rake looked her over-high heels, skirt, thin tights, she didn't really match the surroundings. "Look, wait here."

"Where you going?"

"I'll be back, just wait."

And Rake found himself wandering through the woods looking for wood. There was enough acidic orange city glow that it wasn't dark, and he knew the woods well enough that he knew where the trees had been cut down.

And he was lucky and found a load of local free papers dumped by a lazy paperboy. He carried that all back to Helene. He knew she'd been crying by the mess she'd made of her make-up, but decided not to tell her.

"Here," he said, handing her the papers. "Start tying that into knots."

She frowned. "What for?"

"For the fire."

"Oh." She grinned. "Good idea."

In front of the dead tree was a little hollow of land. It was largely ash, with some half-burnt wood, and had a few beer cans around it—they weren't the first people to think this was a good spot to sit and drink.

Rake piled the wood into a vague pyramid shape, like he'd seen on TV at some point. Then he put all the paper Helene had knotted underneath it. Knotting newspaper had been a task he'd had to do a lot as a kid. His parents had had a coal fire in the front room. It was cheaper than central heating, but it was technically illegal to burn coal in London, so they had to buy 'black potatoes' from round the back of the greengrocers.

"What are the knots for?" asked Helene.

"It makes it burn slower."

"Oh."

Rake lit the fire. "You ain't drank all the vodka yet, have you?"

She shook her head and passed him the bottle.

The fire caught and Rake kept feeding it. They drank and even ate the mince pies Helene's mum had cooked to take to the party.

Rake looked at his watch and took a swig from the vodka bottle. "To 1997," he said.

She took the bottle back. "To next year," she replied,

and then took a swig. "It's gotta be better than this one."

"Yeah."

"This time next year, I'll have been at uni for three months."

"Yeah."

"Fuck," said Helene, looking at her watch. "It is fucking midnight, and I gotta be on the train to work in eight hours."

"Look at it, just sort of squatting there."

"What?"

Rake stood up and pointed at Plumstead, just a few orange lights in an ocean of darkness. "Plumstead, it's a fucking shithole." Rake wavered. The vodka seemed to have gone straight to his feet, so that when he'd stood up his heart had pumped it all back up to his brain. "I hate that fucking place."

"Me too. I can't wait to leave."

"Yeah, me either."

"It's a shit place, y'know? I can't get a fucking job, my fucking girlfriend leaves me for a bastard that beats the crap out of her, an' all that seems to happen to me is that I get the crap beaten out of me."

"Lise left you?"

Rake nodded and staggered slightly, then he stumbled heavily back down onto the log and took another swig of vodka.

"What happened?"

"It's Plumstead, you can't live here unless you beat the crap out of people or want the crap beaten out of you." He pointed at the darkened suburb. "It's shit, it's all hidden. Just under the surface, a real shitheap of a place."

"That's why as soon as I finish school, I'm gonna leave, go up London."

"Yeah, well, I'm going to leave too." She stared at him. "Why the fuck am I here? What the fuck am I here for? I got no job to go to—well, there's the Co-op, but I can fucking stack shelves up London if it comes to it."

Rake climbed up onto the tree. It wobbled under his feet, even with Helene as a counter-weight. "I'm gonna leave next year!" he shouted, waving his hand wide. Then he looked at the watch. "This year, this year. Happy fucking New Year, Plumstead, and fuck you!" Rake gave the suburb the finger, then slipped, fell off the log backwards, and crashed to the ground.

"Rake, you all right?"

He dragged himself up. "Fucking tree likes Plumstead," Rake muttered.

"Jeez, Rake, at least you didn't land in the fire. Here, have some fizz to dilute it."

Rake gulped some Coke. It went up his nose and made him cough. He bunged the last of the paper on the fire. The flames leapt high and he lit another of Helene's cigarettes from it and then treated her to a drunken grin.

"You OK?"

"Yeah. Fuck, yeah."

"I think I gotta go, I gotta be at work at ten."

"Yeah, well." Rake offered her the last of the vodka. She shook her head, so he poured it on the fire, making the flames jump blue. "This is nearly done anyway," he said, kicking dirt over it.

Coffee Cup

September, 2008 - Lehman Brothers, Canary Wharf

They were all called into a large meeting hall and told to clear out their desks. Just like that. Like it was nothing.

Rake was nursing the edge of a hangover and felt like he was staggering around under the yoke of it. As he walked back to his desk his boss handed him a white cardboard printer paper box. His boss didn't say anything, but he looked like a sergeant in a war movie.

Rake looked at his desk. He pocketed his iPod, and looked at the gold fountain pen that he never used, but that the clients used to sign their contracts. He went through the drawers—spare pressed shirt, in the box, tie, in the box, fucking cufflinks, the box. A packet of ibuprofen—he gulped two, just in case the pressure behind his eyes was a headache. What else? Documents, no use to anyone, he couldn't even blackmail the fucking company, there was nothing left to take. He grabbed the half a packet of emergency cigarettes and left the rest of his junk there, then, well within his allocated half hour, got out of the building.

Outside were his coworkers, both those well known and those he'd never seen before. All dressed to earn, grasping their boxes, staring like survivors from a shipwreck. And around them the press, photographing.

Rake left. He didn't want to be the fucking poster boy for the crisis. There were no taxis, so he got on the Tube. The other passengers looked him over, taking in his immaculate suit, the fucking box, the vacant expression—they knew him, not who he was, but what he was, they'd seen the news, the photos, the footage.

It wasn't sympathetic looks that he was getting.

He got off at his stop and headed to the escalators. It was odd to be standing on the fucking thing rather than striding up it, odd to be there at all. It reminded him of when he'd first come to London, when a train that arrived every four minutes was some sort of strange miracle; Plumstead had no Tube links, the ground was clay and impossible to dig in.

He walked out of the station, nearly dropping the fucking box as he searched through his pockets for the ticket. Now he found taxis, and he must have at least that much left, but he'd gone back to the beginning, back to riding the Tube, working two jobs, training, fucking chivvying his way up the ladder.

Fuck.

Fewer people stared at him here. Most people that lived in this nouveaux-smart bit of the Docklands were at work. He walked past a coffee shop, and caught his first sympathetic look: a guy in a business suit, Blackberry in hand. Unemployed, hanging out in a fucking coffee shop pretending he had an office, madly trying to network his way to a new job. He raised his coffee cup at Rake in solidarity.

Rake walked on. Past the old docks, now marinas with floating bars. He needed a drink, and the damned things weren't open. He felt like a fucking refugee, some sort of outcast from capitalism, dumped out of his air-conditioned office, holding onto his now-useless possessions as the waters swirled high.

He didn't want to see the doorman, but he did. The fucker greeted him with a cheery, 'Good morning, sir,' as if nothing had changed, as if he couldn't see the fucking box, as if he didn't know what it meant. Into the lift, trying to avoid his own reflection in the brass. His tie was loose and he looked a fucking mess.

And then into the flat. Helene wasn't there. The evidence of her occupation was—cigarette butts in the ashtray, a glass on the sink with the remains of a spiralina-green health-food smoothie in it. He put the box on the table, and then, sick of the sight of damned thing, removed the cigarettes and kicked the box under his bed where he couldn't see it. He'd just poured a large whiskey and lit a cigarette when she walked in, a frothy coffee in hand, and stared at him.

"You're back early." She started to chew on her lip. He hadn't seen her do that since they were teenagers.

He took a large swallow of whiskey, fucking hundred-and-twenty-quid-a-bottle whiskey for easy drinking.

"What happened?"

He reckoned she already knew, it must already be on the news, the fucking bankruptcy of a too-big-to-fail bank couldn't not be the lead story.

He looked her over then. She looked so fucking gorgeous.

"I've lost everything, my job, all my fucking money..." He shrugged. "All your fucking danger money, it's all gone. Everything."

Maybe he should have taken the gold fountain pen as well.

"What happened?"

"Lehman Brothers is fucking bankrupt. There's nothing left. Nothing."

She slowly put the coffee down on the table and paused. She didn't run over to him, didn't say anything. Rake took a drag of his cigarette, and then dropped it in the ashtray. Then he finished off the whiskey in two gulps. She was just watching him, silent, her hands held still and slightly away from her body as if she'd been frozen in time.

"Oh," she finally said.

"So, how's this work?" asked Rake. "You gonna walk out now, or stick with me until I go to sleep or summink and then sneak out?"

"What?"

"Now I've got nothing, I've lost all of it, I'm not gonna keep you, am I? You're not a woman that sticks around when the shit hits the fan, are you? You can go on. There must be someone out there that's still earning. Some fucker's making money out of this, somewhere, there must be."

"That's what you think of me? That's really what you think of me?" She tossed her hair. "Jesus, Rake, you think I'm a fucking gold-digger?"

He looked at her—seven-grand ring, diamond earrings, Mulberry bag under her arm, Jimmy fucking Choos—and tried not to nod.

"Shit, I mean, shit." She ran her hands over her bob. "I earnt my money, OK? And I didn't fucking leave Rich cos he lost all his money, I left cos I wanted something better.

And I thought you might be part of that, and this is what you think of me?"

"Come on, Helene, you're pristine fucking goods, a luxury item, you're not the type of woman to loaf it out in a bedsit, doing her own fucking washing up. Fuck it, the way you look, you don't have to."

"I'm not a fucking whore, Rake, and I'm not a gold-digger, OK? There's a long fucking way from being tempted by cash to selling myself for it. I can't believe this! You know me, or I thought you did. Where are you getting off on this 'you can't do your own washing up' thing? You know where I came from, you know what I am..." She shook her head. "I thought you were different, not a fucking idiot like all the rest."

Rake slumped down on the La-Z-Boy. "So leave then, I'm making it easy for you, don't drag this out."

"Fucking arsehole!"

Rake was staring at the floor, waiting for the sound of the front door slamming. Seconds passed, the time beat like drums on his ears, and then Helene's arms were round him, cradling his head.

"You're a fucking self-destructive idiot, Rake," she said softly.

He finally looked at her. "Don't drag this out, Helene, don't. If you're going to leave me, do it now."

"You're a right fucking idiot, you sound like you want me to go."

He grabbed her hands. "I don't want you to go. I don't." He swivelled to look at her. "But I've lost everything, Helene, everything."

Her eyes wavered.

"An' don't tell me to get another job. This is it, like the end of the world. There won't be any other investment banks hiring, hell, there might not even be any banks at all tomorrow. Who knows, maybe next week we'll be living in a fucking barter economy, civilisation as we know might have collapsed. An' if it ain't, I gotta fucking start again, find a new fucking trade and who knows when I'll ever have money again."

She sighed heavily. "I know," she whispered.

"So—"

She put her finger on his lips and shook her head. "Later, Rake, later."

He stared. She moved herself so she was sitting on top of him and then she kissed him softly. He tried not to wonder if this would be the last time, and instead put his arms around her and kissed her back.

Then he stood and half carried her, half walked her to the bedroom, and started pulling at her clothes. "I need you, Helene," he whispered, stroking her hair.

"I know," she said.

He undid her jacket and her shirt. She was wearing a nipped-in business suit, ready to start work if anyone offered her a job. He pulled off his tie and threw it and his jacket against the wall, pretty sure that he wouldn't wear the fucking thing again. Then he kissed her along the neck and down to her breasts, nimbly removing her bra as he went. He wanted oblivion—the feeling of her, the taste, the smell, her skin under his hands. He wanted the present, not the future, not the past, just to live in this moment only, with her, forever.

She wiggled out of her skirt and started pulling off his trousers, kissing him like she was gasping for air, like she needed him to survive. She moved herself round to climb on top of him, but he turned, rolling her onto her back. Then he was driving himself into her and she was digging her nails into his back, gasping, and he was taking her, taking everything of her, every moment, every feeling, everything.

Exodus

New Year's Day 1997: Rake's House

Rake woke up just as the scrubby, dirty day was throwing up its final flash of colour before it turned into a dirty orange night. When he padded down the stairs, his father shot him a curious look, but didn't get much chance to question him about Helene as the whole family was heading out to the carvery. Rake persuaded his mother he wasn't hungry, and after a half-hearted go at berating him for drinking she left him to it, telling him to eat dry toast if he was too drunk to be a member of the family.

And then they were gone. The house was quiet. There were the soft noises of it settling, the rush of the central heating. He made and ate a bacon sandwich, staring out at the sky behind the houses opposite. It was like ice cream, a chemical pink and buttery yellow. Then the sun finally set, turning the garden into blue shadows.

He dumped his plate and teacup in the washing-up bowl. He had no reason to care if his mum was mad for his not washing up. Then he went upstairs and got out his backpack, one of those tall ones people take camping. He took clean socks from the drying rack, packed the rest of his clothes, including both his favourite t-shirts and his fucking suit he wore to sixth form. He took his Game Boy, a sleeping bag, a copy of *Lord of the Rings* and *War and Peace*. Then a whole load of good tapes and his ancient Walkman. He left most of his books. They were heavy and he could always get a library card.

And that was it. He sliced a couple of cheques out of the back of his old man's chequebook and put them in his wallet with his fifty-quid Christmas money. He took a moment to look around his house—the Christmas tree, lights off at the moment to save electricity, the cards with happy smiling non-denominational snowmen on it. He gave the house one final sigh and then he was gone, locking the door behind him and posting the keys back through the letter-box.

He didn't bother buying a ticket—no fucker would bother checking on New Year's Day—and he sat on the back of a low metal bench, his feet on the seat, smoking as he waited for his train. Plumstead station was deserted and the platform was exposed. You could see the tracks leading off into the distance. One way towards Dartford where the suburbs turned into countryside and the other towards the lights of London.

To Rake, the train to central London was a big deal. It was a whole 'nother country. Their suburbs were like a village. Most people stayed near to where they were born, only heading up town for special days, and here he was, emigrating for good.

His train was cancelled. The next one was due after another forty minutes' wait. He waited. He had nothing else to do. The train from London arrived and then headed off into the night, leaving its few passengers on the station. He realised he was looking at Helene. She yawned. She was dressed in her work clothes, black suit trousers poking out of the bottom of her trenchcoat. She was fiddling around for something in her bag, her ticket maybe, even though there were no ticket barriers. For her central London wasn't a strange and forbidding country, it was her factory, where she stood on an assembly line, doing her bit to lighten tourists' purses.

Everyone else had left the platform by the time she triumphantly pulled her cigarettes out her bag and started to fuck around with her shitty lighter, shaking it impatiently until it finally caught and she lit up. Then she lifted her head and looked right at him.

Rake waved.

Helene trotted up and over the bridge. He watched her progress, too far away to communicate anything to her, too close to look away. It seemed fitting that she would be the only person from Plumstead to see him off.

"Hi, Rake," she said when she was close enough. She climbed up next to him and put her heels and handbag on the seat. "Where you going?"

"London."

"Oh, what for?"

"Forever."

"What?"

Rake took advantage of her confusion to nick a proper cigarette. "I'm leaving." He lit it with his working lighter. "Plumstead. I said I was going, and I'm fucking going." He was talking around his smoke.

"Now? Right now?" He nodded. "Where you gonna stay? What you gonna do? Does your mum know?"

Rake shrugged, feeling pretty damn good, a cowboy riding out of town. "I'll be fine. I'll live off the land, get a job."

"You've not been able to get a job here! You want me to ask my manager? I'm sure we could do with more Christmas staff."

His vision of moseying off into the distance didn't involve meeting Helene every Saturday in fucking Topshop. "I'll find me own way."

"Are... are you sure? I knew you were going to leave, but I didn't think you'd leave the next day."

"Why hang around? What have I been doing? I ought to have fucking left when they chucked me out of school. There's no reason to stay. I'll be better off up town, and at least there I can live as I like, do what I want."

"Oh." She frowned and smoked.

The automated speaker system announced that his train was about two minutes away. He unfolded himself and picked his bag up.

"Rake..." Helene was chewing her lip again.

"What?"

"Can I come?"

He stared.

"Whenever I feel like I'm drowning, when I feel like I'm going under, you're there to save me. You always have been."

He dropped the cigarette on the floor and then scuffed it out. The train announcer told them where the train was going in its mechanical voice, and he could see the lights up the track.

Helene stood up and smiled. "After all, there's nothing here for me either."

"Helene, if you feel like you're drowning, you need to learn to swim by yourself."

The train arrived in a rush, a whoosh of air and light, then staccato metallic bangs as it came to a halt. There were shrieking beeps as the doors opened. No one got off. Rake turned and got on.

He paused to look back at Helene as the doors shut. And then, with a jerk that nearly knocked him off his feet, the train took off into the night.

Jim

2008: Rake's Penthouse

Tragically, sex doesn't stop time and no matter how much Rake didn't want to move on, he had no choice. When they were spent they lay there smoking for a while, not discussing anything, not ready yet to face the world. And then Rake decided it was well past time for lunch. He didn't normally eat much in the way of lunch at the office, but better to make lunch than calculate how much poorer he was than yesterday.

He pulled on his trousers and shirt and headed to the kitchen. Helene followed, wearing his robe and looking damned sexy in it.

"You don't want to go out?" she asked. "I only got enough food for me."

Go out there and face the news, the papers, the fucking raised coffee cup of solidarity?

"I'll only end up in a bar," he muttered.

She raised her eyebrows and nodded.

He opened the fridge. "Eggs... And spinach." *What the hell did Helene eat?* "Omelette then."

"Make mine an egg-white only."

He stared at her and then went through the cupboards. There was, of course, hardly anything. Rake was happy to find half a chorizo sausage.

Egg yolks, spinach and chorizo. Yum.

"I guess I'd better get changed," she said.

Rake grinned. "Why? You look great in that."

She smiled, but sauntered off to the bedroom anyway.

Rake separated and whisked up the eggs. The ringer downstairs for his door buzzed. He stared at it: there was nothing that he wanted from the world outside, no one he wanted to see. He put a pat of butter in the pan.

It rang again. Probably a fucking salesperson.

Rake started cutting up chorizo. He didn't know what to do with spinach, it wasn't something he would eat through choice. He sort of hacked at it. Manky, wilted leaves; Helene could have all of them.

There was a crash as his front door slammed open and he found himself face to face with Cezek.

"You cunt!" Cezek pulled a flick knife out of his suit pocket.

"Fuck." Rake realised he had a knife in his hand as well, and waved it at Cezek. "Look, back off, OK? Just calm down."

"Calm down? You lost me five fucking mil!"

Not now. Not in front of Helene. Please not in front of Helene.

"Fuck's sake, Cezek, not here, OK? I've got a woman here."

"You think I care about that, you fucking cunt?" Cezek turned and booted Rake in the chest. Rake fell back against the work surface. His knife clattered on the tiles.

"I'm gonna fucking kill you, cunt." Cezek dropped the flick knife on the work surface and drove his knee into

Rake's forehead. Rake bashed his head on the kitchen cupboard and his consciousness swam.

"Rake!" And Helene ran into the living room area.

Cezek paused.

"Helene?" he mouthed. He turned his back on Rake and walked into the living room. "Helene?" he said louder and then she looked at him, recognising him for the first time.

Cezek looked her over, taking in the black silk dressing gown, her rumpled hair, Rake's similarly crumpled clothes. Rake stood. Cezek looked at Helene's engagement ring and then back at Rake. "I thought you said you didn't know where she was, you hadn't seen her?"

"So I fucking lied, all right?"

Cezek just turned and stared at Helene, his mouth open.

"Hello, Cezek," she said. "Been a while."

"Yeah."

"You all right?"

"Uh, yeah. Yeah, I'm fine, y'know." He grinned. "On the up and up, y'know?"

She sighed and tilted her head to the side. "Look, you needn't take it out on Rake. It's not his fault, you understand? The whole fucking system's coming down, but at least you still got your bricks and mortar. Some investors have lost everything. Rake's lost everything."

Cezek frowned in confusion and then nodded. "Oh, the money. Yeah, fuck the money. I'll make more, not a problem. Now's the chance to strike. I lost, but some lost bigger so I'll take their slices of the pie..."

She nodded.

He smiled at Helene. "You're looking good. Real good."

"Thanks."

Rake was starting to feel unnecessary.

"Yeah, real good. So what you been up to? You still consulting?"

Her entire body stiffened and then she shook her head slowly.

"Oh. Well, y'know, I know some people, I could put in a good word for you, if you're looking for employment."

Helene stared. "I..." She glanced at Rake and then smiled at Cezek. "Y'know, I appreciate it, but I got a coupla interviews lined up next week. I know the people, they've pretty much promised it to me already, and it's exactly what I do, so..." She shrugged.

"Yeah. Right." Cezek nodded. "That's good, yeah? Real good. Good."

There was a silence.

"Look, Cezek," said Rake, "as I said, now's not the time. You want to talk, we can talk, but not here and not now, OK?"

Cezek stared at him as if he'd forgotten what he'd been about to do.

"So please go. We'll talk later."

Cezek nodded. "Yeah, yeah, Rake, me old mate..." Cezek's eyes narrowed, then he purposefully relaxed his face and smiled. It looked like it was an effort. "Sure, answer your phone." He turned to Helene. "And you, answer your emails." He grinned. "It's been too fucking long, hasn't it? We should meet up, go out for dinner, chat about old times."

Helene shrugged. "Maybe."

"Maybe? Maybe? Maybe what? Maybe it's been too long? What the fuck?"

She sighed. "Cezek, it's lovely to see you again, but

I'm sure that we've little to talk about."

Cezek just stared.

"Things have changed drastically and I'm just not that interested in rehashing my youth." Then maybe she got some sympathy spare, or maybe it was just the way Cezek was looking. She sighed. "We could perhaps get a drink, sometime, for old times' sake." Something in the way she said that made it clear that that would be one drink, just once. "OK?"

He grinned. "Yeah, sure, whenever, y'know. I'm kinda busy. I s'pose you'll want to catch me when I ain't got my bitches hanging around, heh."

She nodded.

"Right, yeah, well." Cezek looked over at Rake again. "Well, I'll make like the fucking Russian, won't I, then? Yeah."

Helene waved. Somehow she managed to do it sarcastically, waggling each finger in turn, starting from her little finger, right the way up.

"I'll be in touch," Cezek said.

And then he was gone. The door banged shut behind him. Rake picked up the fucker's flick knife and went to stand by the door. He didn't move until the lift dinged. Then he waited for a minute and threw the door wide and looked up and down the corridor.

The cunt had gone.

He turned back and locked the door and wondered what the fuck was the point of a doorman if they let the trash in.

Helene was staring at him. "Isn't that a little bit overkill?" She nodded at the knife.

"No."

She shook her head. "I s'pose you're planning to accuse me of angling for Cezek, are you?" She lit a cigarette and tossed her hair. "I ain't a fucking whore, y'know. I just told him I'd meet him to get rid of him."

"It hadn't even crossed my mind."

She didn't look like she'd believed him. "He's not changed, not one bit."

"You... what do you think happened?"

"What do I think happened? He stayed in Plumstead, that's all. He might be rich but he never left." She looked at him significantly. "We left."

"No, what do you think happened just now? What did you see?"

"What? I heard a crash and ran out. He hit you?"

She hadn't seen the knife? She had assumed it was his. Rake folded the knife away.

"No. He kicked me."

"You all right?"

Then Rake was walking over to her. He wrapped his arms around her and kissed her hair. "Yeah, I'm all right."

He waited a day, and there it was, sitting on his phone like a fucking virtual venereal disease. The text message from Cezek.

'Soz bout the knife was all 4 show calm now lets talk as u said my office 3pm'

Rake was uncomfortably aware of where his phone was all through the day. In the end, he figured if either he or Cezek was gonna die, it was far better it happen away from his flat, away from Helene.

More from habit than armour, he dressed in his sharpest suit. He had Cezek's flick knife in his right pocket and one of his penknives pushed into his left sock.

He felt its weight with every step he took as it rocked there against his ankle. He felt mildly ridiculous.

He got to Cezek's office, a place that was designed to impress by comparison. It was set back on Woolwich High Street, slammed between a pound shop and a Quicksave. Under the red company logo, the glass front displayed various local properties. Inside, there was a clotted-cream carpet, some yukka plants and a fridge of Coca-Cola in glass bottles that were offered to the lodgers as they were being financially raped.

It seemed that Cezek didn't trust men with sales. The estate agents wore snappy red suits with short skirts, a sort of uniform, and fashionable hair, highlighted just enough that you could see their natural colour was dark brunette. One of them showed him upstairs and left.

Cezek's office was a shrine. The best modern furniture had been crammed in with no regard for the austere minimalistic aesthetic it had been designed for, all expensive, as if he was trying to impress his wealth on his visitors without ever thinking of the impression they had already gotten from Woolwich High Street. Cezek's grin launched out of the framed photos on every surface. He was pictured shaking hands with politicians, receiving awards, in front of some of his more choice properties. And not just his grin—his name, Cezek Rulon Hitch, was engraved on framed parchment paper or underlined in newspaper print. The room was dominated by a large red CH, the company logo reproduced and placed opposite the door. He even had a large sofa, presumably in case his visitors were so overcome that they wanted to perform an act of worship.

And the man himself was sitting behind the large mahogany desk, which did nothing for his stature, giving

Rake a look of such hatred that Rake reached into his pocket and grasped the handle of the knife.

Then Cezek smiled. It was a wide smile, like a shark's. It didn't reach his eyes, but then Cezek's smile had never reached his eyes. "Rake, me old china, sit down."

Rake paused, noting that Cezek's hands were on the desk and that there was quite a distance between them, and then sat, taking his hand off the knife, but keeping it close to his pocket. He warily watched the fucker.

Cezek leaned back into the executive chair and sighed. "The money, it's all gone, innit?"

Rake nodded.

Cezek shook his head. "You're a stupid fucker, a right stupid fucker." He spoke wearily.

Rake felt a rush of annoyance and moved his hand away from the knife. "Look, I told you it was gambling, that's what happens. As me old man always said, don't bet what you can't afford to lose."

Cezek narrowed his eyes at him. "And what can you not afford to lose?"

"I already lost everything." *Fuck, not only was he quoting him, he was starting to sound like his old man.* Rake shook his head. "No, I s'pose I ain't. I lost my savings, my job." He shrugged. It was hard being this flippant in front of that fucker, but he was damned if he'd let Cezek see the truth. "But fuck it, I'll just start again. This ain't gonna keep me down."

Cezek nodded slowly. "It's not good for me, y'know? I could really do with that five mil right about now, really do with it." He sighed. "You know, it'll be your bloody fault if me kids end up on the street."

Rake laughed. "As if you got kids."

Cezek frowned at him.

"Have you?"

"Three. Cezek Junior, London and Chardonnay."

Rake stared. "Really? You have children? You ever see them?"

Cezek nodded.

"You're not married. Are you?"

Cezek laughed. "I'm not that fucking stupid! The world's full of hos, and all they want is a cushy life living off me." He leaned forward. The chair creaked under his weight. "Everyone's always after living off me." He threw his hands up as if he were launching a balloon in the air. "But what am I s'posed to do, let my children be dragged up in a council flat, as if they ain't got a fucking father?" Rake just stared. "Nah, they're fine, their mothers don't have to want for nothing."

"Oh."

"So," said Cezek, "that's enough of the pleasantries, let's get to how you're going to make this up to me." His eyes glittered like cubic zirconas.

"You what?"

"You lose me five fucking mil just when the bottom's falling out of my market, that's about six months' mortgage on a few of me empty properties, that is. I could do with that right now. I gotta lose them houses at a loss now, you see?"

Rake nodded.

"It's not fucking good. Me business is suffering, I'm not making enough to cover what I gotta pay, and at a time like this, you lose me my fucking money."

"I'm sorry, mate, I really am." Rake was surprised to find that he was being honest. "But it ain't my fault. You knew you were gambling, and my investments were good. I didn't know that the entire bank was going to sink underneath me, did I? If the fucking government had intervened like they said they would've, then all my investments would still be gold."

"I don't give a fuck about that shit, do not give a fuck at all. All I want from you is a favour."

"A favour?"

"Yeah. I got an order for something, I want you to pick it up for me."

"What?"

"Some charlie, you follow me? I want someone I can trust to not go to the pigs to pick it up for me." He smiled. "Normally I go myself, but I gotta go to court at four about some fucking repossession case, nothing major even if I lose, but I can't not turn up, can I?"

"You want me to run drugs for you?"

"Not run 'em, just drive to Dartford and pick 'em up, that's all."

Rake stared Cezek out. "That's it?"

"Yeah, that's it. I need a favour at short notice, OK? An' I think to myself, who can I trust to not screw me over, who owes me a tiny little favour." Cezek was staring at him, his eyes flat and empty like a shark's. "You follow me? OK, maybe it is gambling, and OK, maybe I knew that, but maybe you still fucking owe me."

"Oh."

"Really, I'm doing you a favour. Helene said you've lost everything. How you gonna pay your rent? How you gonna keep a girl like that wearing your ring with no fucking cash?"

Rake stared at Cezek. "You..." *Shit, he wasn't really going to go along with this, was he? He hadn't fallen so low that he was going to be a glorified courier?*

"You do the deal for me, I'll bung you five percent."

Rake worked his mouth open and shut. It was dry. He needed a fucking drink, not the fucking Coca-Cola. "Five percent of how much?"

Cezek smiled. He knew when he'd chased down a deal. "Two mil. You fucking need me to work that out for you, or are you still enough of a banker that you can work out your fucking percentage?"

Rake ought to have walked out of the office. If he had any dignity then all Cezek should have seen was his retreating back. But all he could think of was the vision of Helene, her perfect hair tied up, washing up in a crappy flat. Sure, she said she was from that, but why the fuck would she stick around there? The last thing he wanted to lose was her. And the last thing she wanted was to return to Plumstead. Rake reckoned that a slummy flat in Welling would be close enough to the same thing.

"That's it? Just drive up there and get you some drugs?"

Cezek leant back in the chair and grinned. "Yup."

"What the fuck you want two mil's worth of drugs for? Don't you need that money?"

Cezek shrugged. "I'm struggling, yes, I'm losing some houses, yes, but I'm not in the position where I have to pawn my stuff or quit my fucking vices."

"Two mil..." Rake frowned. "You're not dealing, are you?"

Cezek laughed. "You think I'm doing that on the side? Fuck's sake, do I look like Seth?" He shook his head. "No, that's for me an' my friends. I gotta entertain, ain't I?"

"Oh."

"I get a lot each time. That's maybe a year's worth. I don't like mixing with fucking drug-dealers, y'know?" He mimed spitting, but obviously didn't gob on his own carpet. "Scum of the Earth, they are."

Rake stared miserably at Cezek's desk. He didn't want to work for the fucker, but...

"You are gonna pay me cash, right? Not fucking drugs."

Cezek nodded. "Didn't think you'd know what to do with the drugs. You'd probably fucking lose them. Or bet them on a three-legged horse."

Rake paused. "Tell me, Cezek, what the fuck is going on?"

Cezek raised his eyebrows.

"Yesterday you were about to stab me in front of Helene—"

Cezek narrowed his eyes.

"—I don't want her seeing that shit, not her, an' now here you are, trying to help me out. How the fuck do I know you're not trying to frame me?"

"Don't you fucking call me a liar, Rake!" Cezek was up and out of the seat, fists clenched. "I don't lie. I never lie, every fucker knows it. So if you don't want to be kicked down the fucking stairs, I'd suggest you shut your mouth, OK?"

"Calm down, Cezek, OK? I didn't mean to imply you were lying."

"Don't fucking call me a liar. I don't put up with that shit, specially not from someone who just lost me five mil of my money, an' here am I, trying to help that fucker out. You think I ain't got no other mates I could bring in on this? Hmmm? You really think that just cos we drank together when we was kids that I ain't got anyone else I could trust? That there aren't any other fuckers that would be happy to make fifty grand?"

"A hundred grand."

"A hundred grand, whatever, I ain't the fucking banker here, am I? But here I am, helping out my wanker of a banker, and why?"

"Yes, why?"

"Not for you, you stupid fuck. For Helene. Fuck knows what she sees in you, but she seemed pretty damned happy there in your flat, didn't she? Pretty damned happy. An' is that why you didn't tell me where she was, cos you was banging her?"

Rake nodded slowly, watching Cezek and wondering what he felt for Helene.

"Well, y'know, we were tight... once... an' I don't want to see her married to some shitheap scabber sitting there on the dole, an' I think to myself, Rake, he is a wanker, but he ain't all that bad. Maybe when he pulls himself up by the arse an' gets himself another job where he can lose other people's money, then maybe he'll look after Helene, cos she don't need no crappy life, y'know? She's had it bad enough already, ain't she?"

Rake was staring, open-mouthed.

"No, she deserves better." Rake looked at his shiny loafers. "She deserves better than me, anyway."

"Damn right!" Cezek's eyes were wide and crazy-looking. "But, y'know, she's chosen you, hasn't she? Women are strange sometimes, they make weird fucking choices"—he shrugged—"but if that's her choice, well, I don't want to see an old mate on the fucking dole, that's all."

"Me either."

"An' y'know, a hundred grand ain't enough, it's just enough to get you started. I don't think Helene's cheap enough to roll over for a man worth only a hundred big ones."

"Yeah..."

"But here I am, giving you a chance outta the goodness of my heart. Many people wouldn't even see you if they were in my position, but here am I. Fucking Jesus Christ himself wouldn't help you out if he saw you begging in the street, but I call you up an' offer you a job, an' what do you do? You throw it back in my face and call me a liar."

"Jeez, Cezek, calm down, OK?"

Cezek sighed and straightened his tie, not that it was loose. He slowly opened his fists and placed them flat on the blotter in front of him. It looked like it was an effort. "Look, you want this job, or what?"

Rake hated himself at that moment. "Yeah," he mumbled.

"Good."

"Cezek, y'know, I'm doing this to help you out, OK? Because, although it's not my fault, at all, I do feel kinda sorry about it."

Cezek laughed. "You're a fucking cunt, Rake, a right fucking cunt."

He threw an old sports bag over to Rake. "Here's the deal. Take that to Dartford, go to the Green Man pub, and ask to see Jim upstairs, got that? You gotta say that so they know you know what's what."

Rake nodded, it was fucking obvious.

"Don't fucking open the bag. I already counted the money, an' I don't think you got the maths to manage it."

Rake scowled at him.

"And here's fifty k of your money," Cezek passed an envelope over. "You get the rest when you return, got it?"

Rake opened the envelope and ran his fingers over the edge of the pink fifty-pound notes. They felt so familiar, so beautiful, like the pages of a well-loved book. "Yeah, when should I go?"

"They're expecting you at around seven, so don't drink all your fucking pay, OK? The fuzz'll pull you over if you can't drive straight."

"I won't fucking drink."

Cezek grinned. "Good."

Rake pocketed the money.

"An' that concludes our business, so get the fuck out of my office, cos I'm still irate, OK?"

"I'm leaving."

Rake paused at the door and glanced back. Cezek was smiling smugly, rocking back on his heels, his hands in his pockets, and Rake realised that the fucker was enjoying seeing him pander to him.

One hundred thousand would keep the bailiffs out for a while. And what choice did he have?

Rake turned and walked out of the office.

The nearest pub was two minutes round the corner. Rake walked past that one, and then found himself at the bar of the next one. A double whiskey, with a double whiskey chaser. Then another. And then another. Then back on the train, kicking the fucking bag down the carriage. A change to the DLR where he stood out—less crummy old sports bags here. He stopped in the pub by his house for a few more whiskeys with whiskey chasers. Then his flat, his parking space, an' his choice between the Maserati and the fucking Ferrari. He threw the bag in the passenger seat of the Maserati and reversed out of the space at six pm. He would have to drive like a fucking Grand Prix driver to get to Dartford in time.

Jim

At seven-thirty he screeched to a halt in some chavvy carpark in Dartford town centre. He'd gone for the one where it looked least like his car would be keyed. And then he strolled to the pub. It was a dark and seedy joint, full of professional drinkers and the sort of professionals who got paid cash in hand. They served manky cheese rolls to help dilute the beer, and the beer was rough and badly kept from the look of it. The locals looked over at him, taking in the suit, the shiny shoes, the short-cut hair, the fucking chunky Rolex.

Rake bought a whiskey and then asked the barman for Jim upstairs. The barman looked at him oddly.

Rake shrugged and downed the whiskey and said, "Well?"

The barman shook his head and grunted, demonstrating you didn't need excellent people skills to run a bar. He tilted his head to the door at the back of the bar and opened it. Rake thanked him and pounded up the stairs, more than ready to get the damned deal over and done with. The door shut behind him.

At the top, there were the toilets and a shut door leading to the upstairs bar area, all painted enough layers of pea-green paint that the pub wood looked like plastic. It didn't look like the lights were on in the bar, but Rake knocked on the door anyway.

"Who you looking for?" called a voice.

"Some fucker called Jim."

The interior lights switched on. "Then come the fuck in." So Rake did.

The lights were the type that hung down from the ceiling and pointed any which way, and they'd been pointed to aim directly at the door. Rake lifted his hand to shade his eyes. "What the fuck is this? Isn't it overkill?"

Then the lights went out and he was bashed on the back of the head. As Rake dropped to his knees, a voice shouted, "Hold it, hold it, get them fucking lights back on."

And then his throbbing head was split by light.

"Fuck! Hold it, boys, there's no fucking way he's a pig."

Rake blinked towards the voice. "Seth, is that you?"

"Rake, what the fuck you doing here?"

"Eh?" Rake dragged himself up and put his hand on the back of his head. It came away wet. He wiped the blood on his trousers.

"You know 'im?" said someone else.

"Yeah, we used to drink together."

Rake sidled to the edge of the room out of the blinding light. Now he could see Seth sitting at a table with a gun next to his right hand and a goon on his left. And off to Rake's right was another fucker, holding a bloodied baseball bat and eyeing him warily.

"Why the fuck didya hit me?" he asked the guy with the baseball bat, who declined to comment. "What the fuck's going on, Seth?"

"You sure he's not the fuzz?" asked the sitting goon.

"No fucking way is Sebastian fucking Rake a copper." Seth laughed. "Look at him, no fucking undercover pig would turn up to a deal dressed like a bloody Hooray Henry!"

Unlike the rest of them, the last eleven years hadn't really changed Seth. He still dyed his hair black, still wore black, still looked pale, and, Rake reckoned, still had a shitload of drugs on him.

"You still dealing then?" asked Rake conversationally.

"Sounds like a cop," said the guy to the left of Seth.

Seth laughed his dry high-pitched laugh. "No cop would be that gormless."

"I ain't a fucking cop, why'd you think that?"

Seth sighed. "You been set up. We was told some fucking undercover investigator had infiltrated Cezek and was coming to the meet."

"What? He is dealing?"

Seth laughed again. "How the fuck do you think he was able to start buying all them fucking mansions?"

"Really? Personally?" The idea of Cezek going door to door with the scag shoved down his pants was amusing.

Seth laughed again, and Rake mused that he'd probably just used up about six months of mirth. "He's too fucking precious to do it himself, the cunt's hands are clean, but he has people all over London, an' no fucker can touch him cos he supplies the filth."

"Oh."

"Have a seat, Rake." Seth gestured at the chair. The guy with the baseball bat loomed over him and looked at Seth, who shook his head. "Chill, siddown, have a smoke," Seth said to Rake, tossing over a rolled spliff.

"You sure? You really sure he's not a pig?" asked the bat-wielder.

Seth nodded and leaned forward. "So tell me, Rake, why the fuck does Cezek want you dead? What you been doing?"

Fuck. "I lost him five mil."

Seth frowned. "You what?"

"Yeah." Rake sighed. "I'm a shit-hot investment banker..." He took a drag on the spliff, not the best idea with a head wound, but in the circumstances Rake reasoned it didn't matter. "Until two days ago, I was a shit-hot investment banker, and I had some of his money invested, and when the bank folded it was gone."

"That's it? Five mil? The fucker was gonna kill you for that?"

"Yeah, jeez."

"Seems outta character. It's never money, it's always about respect with him. It's not like you've been dipping your wick into any of his scabby bitches."

"Hardly. The only tail I've had recently has been Helene's."

Seth stared at him. "Helene? Our Helene? You're fucking her?"

Rake nodded.

"Fuck. And Cezek knows this?"

"Yeah, he found out last time the fucker tried to kill me," Rake muttered. *Fuck, once ought to be enough to give someone a clue.*

"Jeez, and you lost him his money as well? Shit..."

"Yeah."

Seth nodded his head. "Well, you're in a right fucking situation, and no mistake."

Rake nodded.

Seth leaned back and lit himself a spliff. "What you drinking?" he asked Rake amiably.

Rake stared. "Whatever passes for whiskey in this shi-thole. And some ice in a tea-towel."

Seth nodded at baseball bat. "Double whiskey. In fact, bring the fucking bottle."

The guy dropped the baseball bat by the door and headed downstairs.

"So what did Cezek tell you?" said Seth. He didn't offer anyone a puff of his dope.

"Pick up two mil's worth of coke and I get five percent."

"Two mil?"

Seth nodded and the guy to his left picked up the bag and went through it and started pulling out and counting notes.

"I'm gonna kill that bastard," said Rake. "I'm gonna smear his head across that fucking ugly office of his."

Seth chuckled. "Calm down, mate, calm down."

"Calm down? The fucker tried to have me killed, if you hadn't recognised me, it'd have bloody worked as well."

"Cool it, Rake, cool it. Being rash with that fucker ain't a good idea at all."

Baseball bat had come back with a half-full bottle of whiskey and the ice bucket from the bar. He had a bar towel over his shoulder and divested four dirty short glasses out of his pockets.

Rake wrapped the largest lumps of ice up in the bar-towel and held it against the back of his head.

Seth poured him four fingers of whiskey and shared the rest of the bottle between himself and the others. He used the tongs to put a single piece of ice in his whiskey. The baseball bat-wielding guy eyed Rake warily, and declined to drink his drink. Rake knocked half of his back in a gulp.

The counter had lined up all the notes. He lifted his head. "Nah, fucking five hundred thou, as usual."

"What?" asked Rake.

"The normal guy gets five hundred thou's worth of coke once a month, not two fucking million," explained Seth, sipping his whiskey.

"Oh. Shit." Rake knocked back the rest of his whiskey. "The fucker thought I wouldn't do it for that."

Seth shrugged. "Beats me why you'd trust him at all."

"I was unemployed, I lost all my money when the bank went down, what the fuck was I s'posed to do?"

Seth grinned, showing that he hadn't bothered to avail himself of NHS dentistry. "Exactly what the normal guy does."

"What?"

"Ring him up and arrange a meet, tell him you got the drugs, and get the rest of your cut."

"Are you crazy? The fucker tried to kill me! I'm having nothing more to do with him!"

"Yeah? You think that'll fucking save yer? He'll just come for you when you least expect it. You'll be strolling up Shaftesbury Avenue fucking shopping and blam! There you are, your brains splattered all over Helene's nice new shoes, fucking mugging gone tits up, happens every day, no fucking cameras... tragedy, front page of the *Mail* and Cezek, the fucker, will be there to comfort her before her boyfriend's body is cold." Seth sighed. "Again. And this time, I don't think she'll manage to get away before she's Mrs fucking Hitch, you see what I'm saying?"

"Yeah," said Rake. He grabbed the drink in front of the baseball player and downed it. "Fuck."

Seth shook his head at Baseball Bat, who was understandably unimpressed. "Let 'im be. Fucker's just had a presentiment."

Rake eyed Seth belligerently.

"But how about this? I'll get my bosses to tell fucking Cezek that the message didn't get here in time. He'll think the deal went ahead as usual."

Rake nodded.

"He don't know I'm working down Dartford way, he's too fucking posh to bother talking to his old mates now."

"Good bloody thing for you," muttered Rake.

Seth grinned. "So here's what'll happen. You arrange a meet with Cezek, somewhere public, like Hyde Park. Pawn all your shit, sell the lot, bung the money somewhere safe abroad."

"Shit."

"I'll come along to the meet, keep an eye on him. We both know what that fucker is capable of."

Rake nodded.

"You bring Helene an' stroll around like couples do of an evening."

"Bring Helene? Are you crazy? This ain't a fucking reunion! I don't want her in danger. I want her well out of it."

"Think about it. Cezek won't do nothing if Helene's there. The last thing he wants is for her to know the fucking truth, so he'll play nice."

Rake shook his head. "Fuck."

"An' if Cezek's playing nice, then you can get the rest of your money, and then you can fuck off to the Continent and lie low. Cezek will come after you if you're in London, but there's no way he'll follow you abroad. The fucker thinks Scotland's a fucking foreign country."

"Technically, it is."

"Cezek wouldn't know that. I don't think he's ever been outside the fucking M25."

"I should kill that cunt."

Seth shook his head. "You want a life in jail? No, leave it, there'll be other times, other places, other ways." Seth grinned. "Sometimes, with revenge, you gotta wait til the fucker's served up to you on a silver platter, you know what I mean?"

Rake nodded.

Jim

"An' now he's not on a platter for you. He'll be expecting you to do something dodgy, so if you an' Helene act normal, so he thinks you really don't know, you'll have a chance at fucking him over later."

"Yeah, good idea."

"Cool. I gotta explain all this to my bosses. I think they'll go for it. They don't like people trying to dick them over."

"Fuck, yeah."

"After all, a fucking hit like this costs more than fifty grand."

Rake stared at him and Seth grinned.

"Assuming you still have your cut in your pocket."

"Fuck," said Rake. He put his hands to his temples and wished it was a week ago. Then he looked up at Seth. There was a difference since they were kids—the guy was still anaemic and thin, but he'd stopped wearing eyeliner. "Why do you think he's doing this? You reckon it's Helene?"

Seth shook his head. "Fuck me, Rake, what the fuck did they do to you up town? You used to be smart."

"Oh."

"Course it's fucking Helene, it's always been about Helene."

Rake drove out of Dartford first. He wanted to be somewhere he felt kinda safe, so he ended up turning off the A4 and parking outside his dad's flat in Plumstead. He dialled Cezek on his mobile. The fucker didn't answer, so Rake, thinking that he should have expected Cezek to not answer a phone call from a dead mate, got out of the car and rang the doorbell.

"Hi, Dad," he said.

His dad smiled. His rheumy eyes were tilted down at the corners, his nose and cheeks were florid.

"Seb, long time, no see. Everything OK?"

Rake nodded.

"Tea? Or would you prefer a whiskey?"

Rake didn't want to encourage him. "Tea, Dad. You mind if I use your phone?"

"No, not a problem." And his dad pottered off to the kitchen. His strength had gone, turned in on itself. A lifetime of lifting and carrying had left him with arthritis in the knees, a bent back and gnarly hands.

Rake punched Cezek's number.

"Hello?"

"Hi, Cezek." Rake tried to inject some warmth and friendliness into his voice by pulling a grin so the fucker'd hear it in his voice. It was a rictus grin, he could see it in the mirror on the wall. "It's all done, we should meet."

"Who is this?"

"Rake, Sebastian Rake."

Rake found himself staring at the mirror in front of him. He was no longer grinning, rictus or otherwise.

"You... got the package?"

"Yup."

"Oh. Well, yes, we should meet. I'm busy at the moment, a lot of shit's come up, y'know. Tell you what, I'm throwing a party in a coupla days, y'know, to keep people's confidence up or summink. Helene's got your invite, we can meet there—"

"That won't work for me. I ain't bringing this shit to a party. Let's meet beforehand, Hyde Park, by the cafe."

There was a silence whilst Rake listened to the crackle of the phone line.

Finally: "OK. We'll meet there, seven pm. My party starts at nine. You can get a taxi there."

"Whatever."

"Fine then."

Rake hung up and then texted Seth the arrangements. When he looked up, his dad was holding a couple of mugs of tea and staring at him.

"You're not in any trouble, are you, Seb?"

"No, Dad, nothing doing." Rake gestured towards the living room. He sat on the threadbare sofa. He didn't often visit. He hated the feeling of the place.

His dad handed him his mug of tea. He took a sip—hot, strong enough that he felt the tannin filming on his teeth.

"Fuck it, Dad, pour us a stiff one, would you?"

There was no surprise on his dad's face, just a shade of relief. He slunk off and returned with a bottle and then poured two generous doubles into two unclean glasses scattered around the living room.

Rake took half of his in a gulp. His dad did the same. They had that in common. His dad topped them both up.

"I'm gonna be leaving town for a while," said Rake.

"You're in trouble, aren't you?"

Rake nodded. "I lost everything. My job, my money, it's all gone."

His dad nodded. "I seen the TV. All them poor bastards out there with boxes. That was your bank, weren't it?"

Rake nodded.

"I don't understand this. I thought banks was safe, I thought it was a job for life."

"No such thing anymore."

"What you gonna do now?"

Rake shrugged. "I'm leaving the country. Gonna try

somewhere else. Maybe Frankfurt, I don't know."

"Leaving? How long for?"

Rake shrugged. "Maybe forever this time," he muttered. Then he knocked back most of his glass of whiskey. His dad was staring at him with bloodshot eyes as Rake refilled his glass and poured out another for his dad. "Who knows."

"Don't do nothing stupid, you hear? There's no need to take things too seriously." His father worked a dry tongue around his mouth. "I seen the TV. Bankers throwing themselves off buildings, burning their houses down. Don't you go an' do nothing like that. It's just money, Seb, you got that? You're still young."

Rake laughed. "I'm not fucking suicidal." *Homicidal, yes.* "I'll make the money back. Not to worry, Dad."

His father was watching him suspiciously.

As much as to change the subject as to argue, Rake said, "I'm seeing someone."

"Properly? You finally decided to stop fucking around?"

Rake nodded.

His dad smiled. "That's good, I always thought what you needed was a good little woman to keep you home at night."

Rake laughed. That didn't sound like Helene. She was petite, but not really what you'd call a good little woman.

"Who knows, Dad."

"Well, what's she like?" His dad poured them both more whiskey.

"You know her. I'm dating Helene."

"Helene? That little chit of a girl?"

"Yeah."

"Oh, I s'pose I met your mother when I was seventeen..." He stared off into the distance for a moment and Rake looked round the flat. The large expensive TV that Rake had bought his dad for Christmas sat oddly with the rest of the cheap furniture. "Maybe it was a good thing to wait a bit, find your feet."

Rake reckoned that the last thing he'd done was find his feet. He gulped his whiskey and then was surprised that the glass was empty. He poured some more and felt guilty as he finished off the bottle.

"You seen your mother? You told her any of this?"

Rake rolled his eyes. "Dad, I don't visit her if I can avoid it." He shrugged. "She'll find out I'm gone when I don't turn up round Christmas."

"You should see her, she is your mum."

"That's irrelevant. So don't worry about me, I'll be fine."

His dad looked like he knew he was lying. Rake finished off his whiskey and stood up.

"One thing though, Dad, you remember Cezek?"

"Right piece of work, that one."

Rake snorted. "If he comes round here, don't answer the door, just lie low and call the police, you got that?"

"Why would he come here? What've you done?"

Rake shrugged. "He had some money invested with me. It's all gone and you know what that fucker is like."

"It ain't worth it, son. Just leave her with that fucker, he's too rich and too strong to fight."

"You what?"

"You're thinking with your balls and not your head. Just tell her to go back to him and leave it well alone, you understand?"

"Jesus, Dad, you just want me to roll over and let that fucker get everything he wants?"

Jim

Rake's dad nodded. "Better to be around to fight another day. If that fucker takes against you, how you ever gonna get a job?"

"Fucking hell, Dad, I ain't no weakling, I ain't gonna give up just like that."

His dad was staring at him. "Plenty more fish in the sea."

"Yeah, being eaten by sharks, you think that's what Helene wants? She wants me, not him, and I'd die before I left her to him."

"He's a bad one, that one, a real bad one."

"I don't give a fuck!" Rake threw the whiskey glass against the wall.

They both stared at the shards on the floor and the dripping amber liquid.

"Sorry, Dad." Rake sighed. "But I ain't backing down on this, and I don't need no advice from you telling me what to do, OK? I ain't walking away this time, OK?"

Rake's dad said nothing, he just worked his mouth open and shut, leaving a bubble of spittle at the corner.

"Look, I gotta get something, I'll be back."

Rake left the house and walked over to the car. He grabbed the sports bag out of the boot and went through the glove compartment, pocketing some cigarettes and a few lines for his own personal use, left from when he could afford personal use.

He walked back in to find his dad muttering around a limp roll-up and shaking his head, even though there was no one there to shake his head at. Rake tossed the car keys over. "For you. You can keep it if you want, but probably better to flog it, that thing's worth quite a bit."

"You what? You leaving me your car?"

"Yeah, just don't drink the proceeds, OK? Buy some

new furniture and pay the heating bill, all right? Don't spend it on whiskey."

His dad stared at him.   Eventually he muttered, "Thank you, son."

"Right, I'm off then." Rake looped the sports bag over his head.

"Ring me from time to time, let me know how you're doing."

"Sure, Dad."

"Stay outta trouble."

Rake waved and then he was off and out of the house, lighting a cigarette as he walked to the station.

Reunion

2008: Rake's Penthouse, Poplar

Any vestigial whiskey glow was gone by the time Rake had struggled through the drizzly rain from the station to his flat. He ignored the cheery comment about umbrellas from the doorman and went straight up. He walked through to the bedroom. He could hear the shower running, and he kicked the drugs under the bed, where they hit the box of the shit he'd thought worth rescuing from a liquidation sale.

He walked into the main room and up to the bar.

A large measure of whiskey and no ice.

He looked around, trying to ignore the traces of Helene's occupation. She wasn't tidy—there was a pile of job applications on the coffee table, next to a dirty coffee cup and two glasses with red wine residue in them. She'd piled some women's magazines on top of his PS3, the kind that were an inch thick and full of adverts for fashion where the model pulled a vacant expression as if she were a corpse dressed up to look nice.

He swigged the whiskey. What was worth selling here and what could he sell in a hurry? He could bung it all up on eBay perhaps—the widescreen plasma TV, the La-Z-Boy, the art—no, that could go to Christie's. Shit, one day that fucking picture would be worth millions, the day after Tracy Emin got it and couldn't produce such great works any more. Maybe he could put it in storage somewhere. Unlike that frozen head, it couldn't melt. And all the other crap too. His limited-edition DVDs and Blu-Rays, promo stuff from studios, would they be worth even holding on to?

Rake sighed and gulped the rest of the whiskey.

The Ferrari, that'd be worth quite a bit, get rid of that, and sell the flat, if he could...

And that was it. The rest was eBay fodder, maybe. At most, if any fucker was still buying it'd be worth four grand. More than he'd paid for the whole lot, but if every fucker at Lehman was flogging their shit, no one had any money to buy anything.

That was it. The rest of his money, most of which was in his fucking investments, was gone. Shit.

Helene walked out dressed in his robe, a towel over her shoulders and her hair wet.

She smiled. "I was wondering if I should start to worry," she said.

Rake smiled.

"Drink?" said Rake.

"You got any champagne?" She beamed. "I got an interview lined up for next week. I mean, at last. It's been over a fucking month!"

Rake stared and then went through his drinks cupboard. He knew he had some champagne in there somewhere. He grasped a bottle of Tattinger and popped the cork, pouring it out into tall champagne glasses.

"What shall we drink to?" he asked.

She shrugged. "To new opportunities? To money? To being back on the up and up?"

"To new opportunities."

They clinked the glasses.

She smiled and drank the champagne. Her cheeks were pink already from the red wine and the shower.

Rake found his eyes going back to the coffee table. This time he didn't think about how much Appleglass was worth. This time he counted the glasses.

He raised his eyebrows at her.

"It'll be great, a hundred k starting salary, fewer hours than I was doing before."

"What's the job?"

She shrugged. "Nothing too interesting, basically book-keeping, something I could do in my sleep."

"Where?"

"London, of course." She screwed up her nose. "Isle of Dogs, actually. Fuck, I hate East London." She smiled at him. "I s'pose the Docklands're all right, not really East London in spirit."

"Yeah." Rake gulped the champagne. The bubbles burnt his nose like he was snorting cheap coke.

"You're s'posed to sip the bubbly, not gulp it."

He shrugged.

"Oh, an' Cezek's invited us to some fucking soiree. It'll probably be dreadfully awful, but you might be able to network your way into a new job. Perhaps you could con some start-up capital out of his cronies and set up a hedge fund?" She shrugged. "And, y'know, I might be able to find a better job. If there's one hundred-k job going in the City, why not two?"

"Why not two," repeated Rake. His eyes flicked back to the empty wine glasses, the sediment in the bottom, drying purple.

"You all right?"

Rake looked away and out over the city below them, at the skyscrapers, a symphony of shadows and light. This was his Grand Canyon, his Alps, his fucking Ayers Rock.

"Rake? What is it?"

"I think we should leave." He could see her reflection in the window, but he was looking through it, across the river. Up river in the distance was the Wheel, but over the Barrier, directly across the river from him, was Woolwich with Plumstead arching up on the hill beyond, darker still and darker than the city.

"What?"

He turned his back on the window. "I think we should leave the country. I was thinking Frankfurt. The Germans are sensible, if anyone's gonna come through the crisis intact, it'll be them. They'll be first up on their feet, yeah, the Germans."

"Germany? You want to move to Germany?"

"Or Switzerland, lots of work for bankers in Switzerland, no fucker'll find us up in the mountains round Lake Geneva..." Rake tried to imagine living somewhere where the air was pure and crystal clear. "We could ski," he finished weakly.

"Rake, why? I can't speak German and my French is atrocious. Anyway, London's the financial capital of the world."

"What about New York? We could go there."

"Fuck, I mean the Americans have it worse than us, it's their fault. There's no jobs in New York, we'd just get deported."

Rake shrugged. "Tokyo? Hong Kong?"

"Jeez, Rake, what is this? Why do you want to leave?"

"I don't want to leave. I love this city, love it." He even glanced over his shoulder at the lights up river, shining in the darkness like gemstones on a jeweller's display. "Love it."

Helene tilted her head to the side, then sighed, put the glass down and walked over. "It's OK, y'know?" She wrapped her hands around him. "You'll get a job here soon." She leaned back and frowned. "Anyway, you've only been unemployed for two days, Rake, two days. You gotta give it longer than that. It's taken me a month and a half."

Rake slid his eyes over to her, but said nothing.

"But you'll find something, definitely. We don't need to leave."

He stepped back and kissed her on the back of her hands. "What if we did, would you come with me?"

She shook her head gently. "No one needs to leave, Rake."

———————————

Rake was not a fucking idiot. That, at least, was what he told himself. He repacked the drugs into an old briefcase. No pig would stop someone who looked like a respectable member of society and search them for drugs. Or maybe they would—Rake didn't get the best looks on the streets nowadays. He always had to walk past the odd protest and inflammatory posters on his way to the DLR station. His favourite slogan was, 'Bankers laugh, kids cry'. He didn't feel all that much like laughing, which was perhaps why, even with the sharp suit from a little-known and highly exclusive tailor in Brighton and the Thomas Pink shirt, the crazy-eyed protesters eyed him suspiciously as he walked past rather than attacking him with their placards to try and get their £500 billion fiscal stimulus out of his pockets.

But he couldn't bring himself to put Helene on the Tube, even though he used it himself. So they got in a cab and paid the thirty-five quid fare from the Docklands to Hyde Park.

It was pissing it down when the cab stopped. They got out. Helene put up her umbrella but didn't say anything until the taxi driver had pulled away. "Why are we here? I thought we were getting dinner before the party?"

"We will. I just gotta see a man about a deal." He waved the briefcase at her. "It won't take long, and then we can leave."

"A job?"

"A little cash-in-hand work I did."

"Here?"

Rake nodded. They walked down into the park. They weren't the only people walking, but most people were sticking to the main path through the middle. When Rake turned off down the path round the side of the Diana memorial they were alone. Helene looked unimpressed. The cafe was shut. On a summer's evening it would be a nice place to sit out, but on a cold October night in the pouring rain it was shut and dark. The red blinking light of the CCTV camera was the only sign of commerce.

Rake was getting soaked. He fingered the knife in his pocket and looked out at the trees. He thought he saw a black-clad figure standing motionless under one of them, but he wasn't sure.

"You arranged to meet someone here?" asked Helene. She was looking out at sheets of grey water and squabbling ducks on the Serpentine.

He nodded.

"Well..." She looked around them, didn't notice Seth, if it was Seth. "There's no one here."

"We're early."

She sighed. "Let's walk up to the bridge, get out of the rain. You can't go to the party completely soaked, can you? If they can't find us, they can just ring." She started walking. "Although anyone with any sense would seek shelter in this..." She looked thoughtfully at the awnings of the cafe. They would shelter them, but Rake wasn't sure he wanted this recorded. If anything went wrong, well, he would defend Helene, no matter what. And if Cezek got it in the neck, well, it was no more than that fucker deserved.

Rake touched the flick knife handle in his pocket and then took Helene's arm. "Come on, we'll wait under the road, it'll be dryer."

She nodded. They walked up, the black shadow keeping pace with them to begin with. Rake hoped it was Seth and not one of Cezek's cronies. They lost him as they went under the bridge. Rake went and stared out at the mud-coloured rain to see if he could make him out.

"What you looking for? You see this person?" asked Helene.

Rake shook his head.

"Jeez, a cold and wet place to meet. What the hell's wrong with a bar?" She was looking at her heels under the designer silk evening gown. "Fuck, I think my shoes are ruined." She sighed. "The dress is OK, I think... shit, no, there's water staining round the hem. Fuck."

"Sorry," said Rake. He was peering into the rain. It was really hammering it down now, obscuring all vision, turning the park into pink mist.

Helene sighed loudly. "We couldn't have met another

time? I gotta walk into a party like this. I'll look like a fucking reacher who can't even afford a fucking cab."

"No, you look fine, as always," said Cezek.

Almost like horror, Rake turned to see Cezek grinning at Helene as he walked over from the other side of the bridge. He was dressed for a party—white scarf, his coat open to show off a tuxedo and bow tie.

"Cezek?" asked Helene. She looked at Rake in bewilderment. "But..."

Rake walked over and very deliberately stood in front of Helene. Cezek scowled at him.

"Mine, yes?" said Cezek, gesturing at the case, but his eyes flicked over to Helene as he did so.

"Yeah, take it." Rake dropped the case to the floor and kicked it over. "You can keep the case. Worth five hundred quid, that. Consider it a gift." Rake's right hand went into his pocket, he gripped the knife and stepped slightly in front of Helene.

"What the fuck's going on?" she asked.

"Rake's been working for me," said Cezek with a grin. "Y'know, many people wouldn't be so magnanimous, but I thought I'd help the fucker out in his hour of need, despite everything, throw some work his way." Cezek smiled at Helene. "I wouldn't want to see you married to a pauper."

She looked confused.

"You... are engaged, aren't you?" asked Cezek.

Helene looked from Rake to Cezek and tossed her head. "Oh, yeah, that... yeah."

Cezek looked confused, and then a smile broke out across his face as he reached into his pocket.

Rake's entire body tensed and he put an arm out to make sure Helene was definitely behind him.

She stared at him.

Cezek shook his head slightly and tossed an envelope at Rake. It landed in a puddle in front of him. Cezek was grinning.

"You not gonna pick it up?"

Rake gripped the knife and pushed Helene back a little. He stared Cezek out.

Helene hoiked up her dress and squatted to pick up the envelope.

"Helene!" said Rake.

She skipped a few steps away from both of them, opened it and then pirouetted, cash in her hand.

"What the fuck is this? Rake, what did you do?"

"He was a courier for me, y'know?" said Cezek. "That's all. I couldn't trust him with no serious work, could I? I don't even trust that fucker's maths skills."

"Couriering what exactly?" she asked Cezek, her eyes narrowed.

"Look, Cezek, just take your shit and fuck off," said Rake, moving over towards Helene.

Cezek laughed. "Chill out, Rake, chill out." He picked up the case. "You had too much sauce again, right? You'd better be fucking sober for my party. There's people I want you to meet." He smiled. It wasn't a nice smile.

Rake was staring.

"Well, I'll offski then, see you at nine." Cezek picked up the case and gave them both a cheery salute.

It was Helene who saw him first. She turned her head to the side, there was a loud bang and then Cezek gasped, dropped the briefcase and grabbed his chest. Rake stared in stunned incomprehension at the red stain that was spreading across the top of Cezek's dress shirt.

"Fuck," gasped Cezek. He pulled out a gun and pointed it vaguely towards the mouth of the bridge.

Seth strode over. The end of his gun lit up twice, there was a rush of air going past Rake, the sounds echoed with no direction.

Helene screamed. Cezek dropped the gun and fell to his knees, one hand on his chest, the other scrabbling for his gun.

Seth laughed. "You fucker. I've waited years for you to look this fucking panicked. Didn't even know if it were possible."

Helene ran over. "Stop! Please, take this!" She was holding out the envelope.

"Helene," gasped Cezek. The shots had been off target. Cezek was bleeding, but still alive.

"Take this too." She pulled off her engagement ring and held it out. "There's at least forty grand right there. Just leave, go!" Then Seth turned to look at her. His face caught the light. "Seth?" she asked. "What the fuck?"

Cezek's questing fingers finally got a grip on his gun. Rake kicked the gun out of his hand. It bounced off the culvert and went off. The shot sounded loud in the tunnel and ricocheted off somewhere.

Seth ran up to Cezek, lifted him by his jacket and threw him into the water just outside the tunnel. It wasn't more than a foot deep, but Cezek struggled getting back to his feet.

"Fucker," he gasped.

"Seth, stop!" yelled Helene. She started to run over and looked like she might even try grabbing the gun or Seth.

"Yeah, drown, you fucker," shouted Seth, "like you drowned Chad!"

Helene stopped as if she'd been shot. "He... Chad?"

Seth looked away from Cezek's struggle to get to his

feet and nodded. "Yeah, he did it."

She crumpled to her knees, her hands flat on the floor, and just stared at the water.

"Helene," croaked Cezek. He got some purchase and half stood. "It's not what you think..." He slipped with a splash.

Seth started walking slowly down to the water's edge.

"Fuck, Rake, help me!"

Rake put his hands into his pockets.

"Helene?"

She lifted her head to look at him.

"Call the fucking pigs." Cezek struggled back a few steps into deeper water.

Seth laughed.

"The gun, Helene, get the gun!" gasped Cezek. He coughed, blood bubbling up on his lips.

Seth laughed again. "Drown, you fucker." He kicked Cezek square in the chest and Cezek splashed back into the water. Cezek thrashed around, pulling his head above the surface. He made horrible choking, gasping sounds and Rake realized that the fucker was drowning, but in his own blood, not the Serpentine's greasy water.

"You fucker, you right fucker," said Seth. "First you kill my mate. Chad was a straight-up, good, decent geezer, you know? But you, you were planning some hit. I almost told the fucking pigs about you so many times, and a man in my profession don't like talking to the fucking filth. But, no, I thought to meself, I'd bide my time, you'd fuck up some day. And here we are, you fell right into my lap, as if fucking God himself had got down off his pearly throne and flew down through all nine levels of heaven to hand-pluck you, tie you up and drop you in my lap like it's fucking Christmas! I couldn't ask for a sweeter set-up, and the cause of it? The woman that you started all this shit for in the first place." Seth gestured with the gun towards Helene. "Talk about fucking irony. That is just the marzipan-lined icing on the fucking cake. Maybe Buddha and Allah had to help pull that one off! And all that breath you wasted polluting Plumstead's air with your fucking angst over her leaving you. I'd bet you'd be glad of it now. And there she is, she finally knows, you fucker, she knows what you did, and she ain't gonna forgive that shit. I ain't gonna forgive that shit."

Seth glanced at his watch and looked back at Cezek, who'd done his best to wade away from Seth at this point. He wasn't getting anywhere very fast, but he didn't look any closer to death than he had been before Seth's diatribe.

"Dammit, you're still struggling. You can't even fucking drown properly, not even in the name of poetic fucking justice."

Seth aimed this time and shot Cezek twice in the head. Cezek disappeared under the water then bobbed back up, bizarrely still. They watched as he drifted on the water, the rain pounding on his open eyes. Seth pocketed his gun and pushed Cezek back under the water. He didn't bob up this time.

Seth wiped his hands on his jeans and turned and walked up the bank, water dripping off his trenchcoat. "I've been waiting years to do that. Been too fucking long that fucker's got away with it." He grinned at Rake. "Thanks, mate."

"I didn't know you were going to shoot him!"

"Course I fucking was! What exactly did you think I was going to do to him that would stop him from coming after you and trying to kill you again?"

Helene glanced up at Seth.

"Sit us all down at a table in a posh restaurant and mediate a discussion between reasonable adults? Like fuck."

"Fuck," said Rake.

Seth reached into his coat and handed Rake an envelope. "In there is two passports for a Mr and Mrs Smith and two plane tickets bought with a clean credit card. If I were you, I'd get the fuck over to Heathrow, soon as." He nodded at Helene, who was still on her knees, utterly motionless, now just staring at the water. "And take care of her, yeah?"

Rake looked at the passports.

"And, I s'pose, as far as I'm concerned, the coke's yours. I presume you know what to do with it, right?"

Rake stared. "How'm I gonna get it through Customs?"

"Check it in the hold. No one's gonna look twice at a businessman with a fucking briefcase."

Rake looked over at Helene. She hadn't moved. She was now staring at the water where Cezek had last been seen. He hoped he'd be able to get her up and into a cab, but he wasn't certain it'd be easy.

"What about you?" he asked Seth.

"I've killed for them now, ain't I? A fucking made man." He grinned. "I'm on the fucking up and up!"

Printed in Great Britain
by Amazon

58769413R00151